SEDUCTION

Werewolves of Montana series
Mating Mini #1

BONNIE VANAK

SEDUCTION

ISBN: 978-1-941130-11-7

Published in the United States of America.

Desperate to free her family from their evil alpha, curvy werewolf Alexa Grant sells her virginity in a private auction. Alexa has heard nothing good about Jeremiah Jackson Taylor, the Lupine who purchased her innocence. She'd rather experience passion with J.J., the sexy and handsome cowboy who stole her heart when she worked at Aiden Mitchell's Montana ranch.

Alexa doesn't know J.J. is Jeremiah Jackson Taylor, the mysterious billionaire ranch owner who bought her for one night to rescue her from her pack. Determined to prevent another man from touching Alexa, J.J. will tutor her in the erotic pleasures of lovemaking. But when it becomes clear someone at the ranch knows his secret and is trying to pull them apart, J.J. knows he must step out in trust and tell Alexa the truth, or risk losing her forever…

CHAPTER 1

Jeremiah Jackson Taylor had never paid women for sex. But all that would change soon, when he shelled out half a million for a virgin.

Not just any virgin, but Alexa Grant, the only female he wanted in his bed.

"When is she getting here?"

Aiden Mitchell, alpha Lupine of the Mitchell pack, leaned back on the sofa in his lavish office. "Chill out, J.J. She'll be here soon. So, how does my portfolio look? You done yet?"

J.J. peered at him over the top of the computer screen on Aiden's desk. "You chill out. It takes a few minutes to make a million dollars, wolf."

"Not that you'd know anything about it," Aiden drawled. "You've only made a million in the past month."

"Ten."

"Braggart."

Chuckling, J.J. returned his attention to the spreadsheet. His mind clicked like a combine whirling through a wheat field. This was his turf, the land of stock symbols and earnings. He loved this stuff.

Humans, or Skins, as Lupines called them, were amateurs compared to him.

He studied Aiden's portfolio and scribbled notes on a pad. "Not bad. You've done well, followed my advice and avoided sticking to only large cap stocks. But buy this." He tapped the pad. "Stock's gonna split. I got a feeling."

Aiden went to the desk and studied the NASDAQ symbol. "Thanks. I'll call my broker right away. I owe you."

J.J. shrugged. "A deal is a deal. You teach me ranching, I dole out stock advice."

He became wealthy after he'd invented software for cell phones. With that money, he'd then bought and sold Google, Netflix and other stocks before the prices soared. He spoke five languages fluently, including Spanish and Japanese. His ranch in Colorado was a place where he could make his pack feel at home. But the real money was on Wall Street. Aiden had become his good friend after J.J. gave him a million dollar loan nearly interest free. J.J. believed in good business and Aiden had returned the favor by teaching him ranching and how to breed horses.

Footsteps sounded in the hallway. Not the heavy tread of male boots, but a lighter, quicker step. There was anger in that walk. J.J. caught a light female fragrance and he glanced at Aiden, who suddenly went still.

"Nikita," Aiden breathed.

"The one and only, the female alpha of the Blakemore pack?"

"Yeah. My future mate." Aiden gestured to the chair and J.J. headed for the sofa as the Mitchell pack alpha sat behind the desk.

This should be interesting. J.J. propped up a worn boot on the coffee table and settled back to watch.

The oak double doors banged open and a Lupine female stood in the doorway. She had long, dark blonde hair spilling past her breasts and her blue eyes blazed with anger.

"Don't you knock?" Aiden drawled.

"You cut off my supplier for feed, Mitchell, you bastard! The store refuses to sell me hay." She crossed the plush carpet and stood before the desk, her hands fisted. "Are you trying to close down my ranch?"

"You keep postponing the mating challenge sweetie, and I'll cut off a lot more. I'm tired of waiting to claim what's mine."

"I'm not yours."

"Yet," Aiden said softly.

She growled.

"You're so cute when you do that," Aiden told her. He picked up a black, hand-held radio from its cradle on the desk. Static crackled. "Kyle, grab a couple of guys and head to the south barn to load up a truck with the hay I bought."

"Sure thing, Aiden," a deep male voice responded.

Nikita's mouth worked. "I won't go into further debt to you, Mitchell. You already have the mortgage on my ranch."

Aiden set down the radio. "No debt. I always take care of my own, sweetheart."

"So do I." A shadow flashed across her face. She turned to J.J. "Who are you?"

Alpha female Lupine. He could tell by her scent, and manner. Aiden sure had his paws full. J.J. propped up another boot on the coffee table. "The feed supplier."

3

"I've bought hay for years from Bristol's. I've never seen you there!"

J.J. took a deep breath, tried to control his tongue. Alpha females made him a little uncomfortable. "B-b-ought the place a f-f-few days ago."

Her blue eyes rounded. "Why?"

"My f-f-friend here," he waved at Aiden, "n-eeded a f-favor."

He locked gazes with her, daring her to mock his stutter. Let her. Everyone in the room knew who held the real power. Maybe he couldn't talk, but money sure as hell did.

She didn't sneer or laugh. Instead, she bristled. "Do you always buy million dollar feed stores for your friends?"

J.J. shrugged. "Only when they need t-t-o get laid."

Nikita stared at him for a moment, then laughed. It was a rich, warm-blooded sound and suddenly he knew why Aiden was smitten. She whirled and turned to Aiden. "I'll say this for you, Mitchell. You've got balls."

"Sure do. Want to see?" Aiden stood and his hand went for the zipper of his jeans.

She turned back to J.J. "Happen to have a magnifying glass handy?"

J.J. chuckled and tipped his hat to the female. Nikita studied him. "So who are you?"

He took another deep breath. "Jeremiah Jackson Taylor." He could easily state his name without stuttering. "Head of a s-small pack in Durango, Colorado."

Nikita's eyes widened. "As in Jeremiah Jackson Taylor, the reclusive Lupine millionaire..."

4

He gave a modest shrug. "B-billionaire."

"The cutthroat wolf of Wall Street, the obnoxious, arrogant bastard everyone envies, admires and hates?"

He touched the brim of his Stetson. "And y-you are?"

"Nikita Blakemore. My future mate," Aiden said.

"Don't be so certain." Nikita studied him coolly before turning to J.J. "Jeremiah. You don't look anything like those photos I've seen of you. You're very handsome. Only alphas can compete in the challenge for the right to mate with me. Interested?"

Aiden growled deep in his throat. J.J.'s nostrils twitched at Nikita's delicate fragrance and the scent of arousal. Her pulse quickened every time she looked at Aiden. For all her harsh words, Nikita was very interested in Aiden claiming her. The sudden realization made his tongue relax and his throat soften.

He pushed back his hat and shrugged. "G-got another lady in mind."

Nikita's eyes widened. "Who? Anyone I know?"

"Maybe." His guard went up.

"I should find her, take her into my pack. Buy her out as you bought out my feed supplier." Her expression tightened. "Then you'd know what it feels like to be backed against a wall."

J.J.'s inner wolf rose, and his claws came out at the thought of someone taking away his Alexa. But his human side knew how to handle Nikita. He smelled fear beneath her bravado. And he knew what it was like to struggle with pride and dignity when you had absolutely nothing left and someone else held the cards. Never again would he sink to that level of desperation and poverty.

"She's the o-one backed against a w-wall. Reason why I'm getting her out. She hates her a-lpha. He's a manipulative c-control freak."

Alexa hated her alpha worse than she hated Jeremiah Jackson Taylor, or so he hoped.

Nikita's gaze grew troubled. "Then get her out because nothing is worse for a female than a bad male alpha. But what pack? The only crappy alpha I know around here is Daniel North. He's very bad news."

Don't I know it. He's an ass. Once he was not, but then he changed...

"He'd made his money through an auto mechanic repair shop in town," she continued, "but someone opened a new shop next door and forced him out of business. Then he opened a bar and someone put the squeeze on him and got the state authorities to revoke his license. Sounds like that someone wants to ruin him. If I knew the person who did it I'd shake his hand because Daniel North is a bastard who only cares about himself, not his pack."

"You, y-y-ou d-do know him." J.J. sat up straighter, his throat tightening. "Me."

Nikita stared and then laughed. "Good for you. I'm sure your lady friend will be glad to leave Daniel's pack for you. You have to be a better mate."

"Better than me?" Aiden asked and then he laughed at her outraged expression.

"A gnome with warts would make a better mate than you, Mitchell. He'd probably kiss better, too," she told him.

A determined look flashed across the male's face, then Aiden pushed back from his desk and in two giant strides, pulled Nikita into his arms.

As her lips parted in a protest, he covered her mouth with his. Nikita fisted her hands and pushed against Aiden, but then her fingers relaxed and she leaned into the kiss.

J.J. watched. This was the kind of passion he longed for, the mating heat that made male werewolves frenzied with need and females soft with yearning.

Aiden released Nikita and rubbed a thumb along her swollen lower lip.

"Any time you want another one, let me know. You need to be kissed and kissed often, sweetheart."

Flushing, she backed up, her legs connecting with the coffee table. Nikita scowled. "Screw you, Mitchell."

"Not until we're formally mated, sweetheart." He grinned. "You're worth the wait."

"You'll be waiting a long time, Mitchell. Until hell freezes over." Nikita went to the window and pulled back the curtain. "Your men had better load up my truck soon. And I'm paying you back soon as I get the money."

The alpha female frowned as she stared at the gravel drive outside. Doors slammed. She glanced at J.J. "There's a female outside."

Alexa. Finally. His stomach tightened. She was here to sign the papers selling herself to him.

"But she's not alone. Someone just pulled up in back of her."

They joined her at the window, watching Alexa slide out of a ratty red pickup truck. J.J.'s heart raced. Alexa was so pretty, with her lush curves and natural grace. Sunlight picked out highlights of chestnut in her long, curly brown hair and when she smiled, his heart raced. And then an older Lupine with brown hair and a dour look climbed out of a shiny black Jaguar and approached her. A beer belly oozed over his belt.

"Daniel," J.J. muttered.

They watched Daniel grab Alexa by her upper arms and shake her. J.J.'s jaw dropped.

"What the hell?" Nikita cried out.

Claws emerged from J.J.'s fingers as a low growl rumbled from his throat.

Then Daniel flung Alexa to the ground. She landed hard, her face striking the gravel.

A red haze filled J.J.'s vision. Son of a bitch! How dare that bastard hurt his Alexa?

J.J. bolted for the door, flung it open and raced down the hallway, shifting as he ran. His wolf didn't care. His wolf only knew his mate was in trouble and needed him. Halfway down the wide staircase, he leapt over the banister, landing on all fours. Growling, he ran for the door, his claws gouging the thick oak. But his wolf couldn't open the door. Fuck this. J.J. spotted a window and crashed through it, shattering the glass. He raced across the porch and nearly made the stairs. Gonna rip him up, gotta protect his Alexa...

A heavy body, Aiden's, landed on him, pinning him to the porch. He snarled. J.J. struggled to be free, his paws scraping against the wood floor, wanting to sink his teeth into Daniel, make him hurt as he'd hurt Alexa.

Snapping at the one who held him down, he looked up to see a smaller wolf race out the now-opened door, snarling as she headed toward Daniel.

A deep male voice roared. "No, Niki! Don't touch him! I won't risk a pack war on my ranch!"

In wolf form, Nikita ground to a halt before Daniel and snapped at him, but maintained her distance.

"Niki, sweetheart. I need you to calm down. You spill another alpha's blood on rival land and you start a turf war. I'll take care of this. Please," Aiden called out.

Howling, J.J. twisted and writhed, but Aiden had him pinned. Frustrated rage turned to grief as he watched Nikita lope over to Alexa, lick the blood streaming down her lip. Then Nikita shifted back, clothed herself by magick and helped Alexa stand.

"You okay, honey?" Nikita asked.

Gazing at the ground, Alexa nodded. Her shoulders quivered, and he sensed it wasn't from fear, but fury.

"Get the hell off my land, North, before I forget my own rules. I will not attack another alpha on my land and risk a pack war, but I'm sorely tempted to kick your ass. Would be worth it," Aiden told him, still struggling to hold J.J. down.

"You can't touch me and you know it, Mitchell. She belongs to me. My pack, my rules." Daniel gave Alexa a disgusted look. His eyes were pinpoints of brown in a doughy face.

"I'm gonna be nice and let you sign the papers by yourself, Alexa. You're selling yourself, you can sign your virginity away."

He climbed into his Jaguar and drove off in a splatter of gravel and dust.

As Aiden released him, J.J. stood on all fours, his fur bristling. How could a male alpha treat his pack females like that?

"I'll take her inside, get her cleaned up." Nikita hooked an arm around Alexa's waist and helped her up the porch steps. "Come on honey. A little soap and water and a shot of brandy will do the trick."

9

"I don't drink," Alexa said softly. Her voice, so sweet and melodious, tore J.J. apart. Gods, he could sit for hours and listen to her talk. He looked at her bloodied lip and fresh rage clenched his stomach.

"Please, I just need to use the bathroom. No fuss."

"Down the hallway, first door on the left," Nikita told her.

Watching Alexa hurry inside, J.J. shifted back to his human form and clothed himself by magick.

Nikita's blue eyes grew haunted as she looked at J.J. "If she is your lady, then you need to get her away from that fat bastard. Yesterday wouldn't be soon enough. I've seen males like that before and they only get worse."

"I will."

Nikita glanced at Aiden. "Tell your men to deliver the hay to my ranch. I'll put the delivery charge on my tab."

"We'll settle your tab in my bedroom when we're mated, sweetheart," Aiden said, unsmiling.

"In your wet dreams, Mitchell."

When Nikita drove off, Aiden sat on the porch steps. "You owe me a new window."

"You'll get your damned window. Should have let me kill that bastard." J.J. joined him.

"Not on my land. I can't risk a war right now. Not when I have more than 80 males itching for a fight every five seconds because they're horny as hell and need mates."

J.J. clenched his trembling fists, willing his raging beast to calm.

Aiden braced his hands on his knees. "Why did you ruin Daniel?"

"Something that happened in my past. Long story. I don't care to tell it."

His friend gave him a level look. "I don't get it. You're rich, successful and powerful. You never stutter with me. Or Darius or Kyle or any male. And why do you need to buy Alexa's virginity?"

"Alexa is mine. I will not let another male have her, get it? If she sold herself to another male..." he struggled to breathe, "I'd want to tear him apart. The thought of someone else touching her, maybe abusing her, I couldn't allow that to happen."

His friend nodded, his jaw tight beneath the black beard. "I get it. I'm the same with Nikita. That female drives me insane, but if another male wins the mating challenge...no way in hell will I allow that to happen. I don't care what it takes, I will win her as my mate."

Aiden's determination echoed his, yet Aiden couldn't know what it was like to be a successful pack leader and not even be able to hold a ten minute conversation with a female Lupine without sounding like Porky Pig. J.J. had fought hard to become the best—the smartest in his class, then the richest Lupine, the most attentive lover.

But relationships were impossible. How the hell could he hold a relationship when he couldn't hold a conversation with a woman?

Then last month he'd visited Aiden's ranch to take roping lessons under his usual disguise of J.J. the cowhand. During that time Alexa came to cook for Aiden's pack, to fill in for the regular cook who was visiting relatives.

They'd instantly hit it off. Like J.J., she spoke fluent Spanish. He never stammered in Spanish. By the time

11

Alexa left a week later, he burned with the need to have her. But there was one small problem—his reputation as Jeremiah Jackson Taylor, hated by most Lupines for being rich, arrogant and successful.

A week ago, Aiden informed him of a very private auction for Lupines only. Alexa was selling her virginity for $500,000. J.J. had won the bid. No other male would touch her.

A door closed inside the lodge. Aiden turned. J.J. caught the other male's arm. "Hold on. Don't tell her my full name."

Aiden looked down at the hand holding him fast. J.J. released him.

"Why?"

"She doesn't know who I am. Didn't want to overwhelm her with the rich, big, bad alpha role."

"She has no idea you're the one purchasing her virginity? The reclusive, wealthy Jeremiah Jackson Taylor?"

He lowered his voice. "She thinks I'm a cowboy."

His friend stared at him and then shook his head. "Good luck," Aiden said dryly. "Tell her the truth of who you really are. Starting a relationship with a lie is not wise, Romeo."

J.J. flipped him the finger. "Fuck you."

"No thanks. You're not my type."

Alexa walked outside and the males stood. J.J.'s heart gave a painful flip. So pretty. Chestnut brown hair spilled down her backside, nearly to her waist. Her sweet little rosebud mouth was made for kissing and he longed to stroke her smooth, soft cheek and stare into her blue eyes. She had generous breasts and curves for a male to squeeze and hold.

12

Damn, he was smitten.

She saw him, and her face lit up. Alexa's gaze flicked to Aiden, then back to J.J. as she spoke in rapid Spanish. "So that wolf who crashed through the window was you. Are you okay?"

"I'm fine," he said in the same language." He was relieved to see her lip had healed. "Did he hurt you badly?"

Alexa flung herself into his arms. Stunned, he stroked her silky hair as she buried her head against his chest. "Thank you for caring."

"I wanted to rip him apart for what he did to you."

"I'm so glad you're here. But why are you here?"

J.J. hesitated. "I'm representing Jeremiah Taylor when you sign the papers."

"Why? He isn't man enough to do it himself?" She raised her head. Not tears, but anger glittered in her gaze. She switched to English and her voice went cold. "Daniel's an ass, but Jeremiah Jackson Taylor is worse."

J.J. went still, his heart racing. "I run his ranch and I'm authorized to act as his legal representative. What do you have against Taylor?"

"He's buying me like a prize mare." Her beautiful mouth wobbled as she stepped away from him. "The minute Daniel heard Taylor wanted to pay half a million for my virginity, my life became hell."

"But you put yourself up for auction," he said slowly in English.

"It was a desperate gesture to keep Daniel off my back when he kept nagging me to repay the money I owed him. I figured no male would pay half a million for me. Most male Lupines want mates, not one-night stands."

13

She clenched her jaw. "And then Taylor offered the money and Daniel forced me to go through with this."

Fuck.

"Jeremiah Taylor must be a selfish, arrogant male who thinks he can buy anything or anyone. I've heard nothing good about that Lupine."

"Huh," Aiden murmured. "Sounds like you don't like Mr. Taylor."

"I hate him." She drew in a quivering breath. "But that doesn't matter, sir. All I have to do is sleep with him for one night. I can handle one night with the wolf. Are we ready to proceed?"

Alexa ran a hand through her long hair and glanced to the right. J.J.'s chest tightened. Long, brown hair, that looked just like Selena's...the bitch who'd tormented him...

Selena had given him that look when she'd confessed she wanted him. Fifteen years old, still a virgin, he'd fallen in love with her. Selena told him to meet her in the barn at night. In the dark, she whispered for him to undress. He'd stripped naked and then...

Fisting his hands, he followed Aiden and Alexa upstairs.

She's not Selena. But she belongs to Daniel's pack, so how do you really know she isn't working with him?

Outside Aiden's office, Alexa slid her small hand into his and squeezed tight. He forgot about his past and squeezed back.

"I wish I didn't have to do this," she whispered.

Me too. But he could not let another male purchase Alexa's innocence.

Alexa sat at the polished conference table. J.J. sat next to her as Aiden went to find Darius, the pack beta, to witness the signatures to finalize the contract for Alexa to sell her virginity to Jeremiah Jackson Taylor.

"I'm glad Taylor sent you to represent him in this arrangement, J.J." Alexa's lower lip wobbled. "I appreciate having a friend here for support."

Oh darling, I'd do more than that. But first I have to convince you I'm not the ogre everyone says I am.

He spoke rapidly in Spanish. "Why are you going through with this, Alexa? Most female Lupines don't sell their virginity."

"Most female Lupines don't owe their pack alpha $200,000 for a college loan. Plus interest. He gave me the money on the terms that I had to work for him after graduation and put in enough hours to pay him back in monthly installments."

She sighed. "Every time I'm five minutes late, he docks my pay, so I'm always behind. And the interest on the loan keeps going up. If I don't sell my virginity, Daniel will force my father to work on the ranch to help repay the loan. My dad is ill. Daniel will work him to death."

"You could find a mate," he gently suggested.

Alexa laughed, the sound bitter. "Someone like your boss, Jeremiah Taylor? A wealthy, heartless ass?"

J.J. ignored the insult. "What about me?"

She gazed deep into his eyes. "You're so noble and sweet. But I need lots of cash."

"What if I told you I had money?"

"This is the only way Daniel will let me pay off my debt. He wants to punish me for standing up to him. As soon as the deal goes through, Daniel will free me and my family from the blood oath of loyalty we swore to him."

15

Bleakness entered her gaze. "Daniel says the half million will make up for losing us as pack members. My body is all I have left of value."

"Not true." No, you are far more precious, sweetheart. And worth more than a lousy half a mil. You are priceless.

Alexa bit her lip and stared out the window. "But you won't want me after this deal, because I'll be... ruined."

"That's not true," he told her again, softly.

Holy goddess Danu, what a damn dilemma. J.J. squeezed her hand. Gods he hated what he had to do, but admired her courage and strength.

It was now or never. He had to tell her the truth. Easy now. "Alexa, what if I told you Jeremiah Taylor wants you as more than a one-night stand? He's looking for a mate."

She stared as if he'd suggested she tap dance naked on the table. "Me? Why? I have no money."

"He doesn't need your money. You have pure bloodlines and a pedigree..."

"So do dogs who win at the Westminster Kennel Club." Alexa stared at the wall. "I'd rather mate a beagle."

"Give him a chance."

"I don't have much choice, do I?" Her knuckles went bloodless as she tightened her hands on the armrests. "I have to have sex with him. He has all the power. Just like Daniel, he thinks he can control me. But once I fulfill the terms of the contract, no one is ever going to make me feel powerless again."

"He's a decent Lupine. He has money, but..."

"A deal is a deal," she said mockingly. "That's

16

Taylor's catch phrase. He uses his money only to benefit himself."

"That's not true," he protested. "Where did you hear this stuff?"

But then the double doors of the office opened and J.J. tabled the conversation. Aiden walked inside, followed by Darius. The pack beta's mop of black curls tousled as if he'd been riding hard.

Or had been ridden hard, J.J. realized, catching Darius' musky scent of sex.

As both males sat, Aiden picked up the sheaf of legal forms. "Alexa Grant, the alpha of your pack has agreed to have me act as a neutral third party in brokering this arrangement. I have held the funds in escrow and drafted the agreement suitable to all parties."

Alexa looked miserable as Aiden read aloud the terms.

"You have agreed, upon your own free will, to sell your virginity for $500,000 to Jeremiah Jackson Taylor. I need your verbal assent."

"Yes," she said quietly.

"Therefore, upon signature of these documents, and the plane ticket he has provided you, you have 48 hours to arrive at Jeremiah Jackson Taylor's ranch in Colorado. You will spend seven days as his guest. On the seventh night, you will go to his bed and the terms of this transaction will be consummated. The money is held in escrow until the following day, when it will be wired to Daniel North's account." Aiden handed her a letter-sized envelope. "There's a check inside for $2,000 for contingencies, should you encounter unexpected travel delays."

"I don't understand. Why can't I just go there, get this over with? Why the seven day wait?" She gave a bitter laugh as she tucked the envelope into her pocket. "So he can have his medical team check me out, assure him I'm a virgin? Or is he so cruel he wants to torment me?"

"Mr. Taylor has expressed his belief that you are an honest and honorable Lupine and has no reason to suspect your innocence. He wishes you to become comfortable with his ranch and his surroundings, and be granted every courtesy as a guest."

"Treat me as his guest before he makes me into a whore." Alexa pushed a hand through her long hair. "There's one more condition that Daniel insists on."

Anger fisted his stomach as she told them. Daniel would show up at the ranch on the eighth day to personally escort Alexa home.

"He's a control freak." Alexa gave a rueful smile. "He wants to make sure the money is in his account before he lets me and my family go."

She looked at Aiden, who nodded to J.J.

"J.J. is Mr. Taylor's personal representative. He is authorized to make decisions on his behalf. Do you agree to this new term?" Aiden said.

"I agree," J.J. muttered.

Alexa reached for a pen. "Give me the papers, please. I need to get this over with and head back to the farm before Daniel blows a blood vessel. With my luck, it won't be fatal, just make him even meaner."

She signed the papers, and he and Darius signed as well. Then she sat back and looked at the forms with a glum expression.

"Cheer up. He's really not as much of a bastard as you think," Darius said helpfully.

J.J. resisted the urge to kick the beta under the table.

She pushed away the contract as if it were smudged with dirt. "He could pay me two million dollars and it wouldn't change my opinion of him being a selfish, callous hard-hearted jerk. What kind of person actually purchases someone's virginity?"

Damn. Well, darlin', the kind of wolf who wouldn't let you sell it to anyone but him.

Darius began humming "Money can't buy me love." This time J.J. did kick him under the table. The beta winced.

The males stood politely as Alexa rose and stuffed the check into her pocket. She held out a hand to Aiden, who shook it.

"Thank you for agreeing to broker this deal, Mr. Mitchell. I appreciate it. And thank you for hiring me last month to cook for you. You were quite generous."

Aiden's mouth quirked upward the barest bit. "I wish you good luck, Miss Grant. I think you'll find Mr. Taylor is not as cruel as you believe."

Darius nodded. "I think you may even find yourself closer to him than you realize."

J.J. glared at him. One more word from you, Darius, and I'll kick you someplace else.

He didn't like how pale and thin-faced Alexa looked. As they went downstairs, Aiden nodded at the kitchen. "We have coffee and oatmeal cookies which Sam, Darius' mate, has made. Will you please join us?"

The offer of food to seal a deal was traditional among Lupines. But as they sat around the table, J.J. couldn't help but notice how Alexa tried not to gulp down the cookies. Fresh anger filled him. What the hell was Daniel doing, starving the poor female?

He looked at Aiden, then flicked a covert glance at Alexa. "I'm still hungry. Think I'll rustle up some bacon and eggs. Anyone want some?"

Darius set down his coffee cup. "Bacon and eggs at this hour? You nuts?"

This time, Aiden kicked the beta under the table. Darius winced.

"Yeah, make a whole bunch. I'm starved," Aiden told him.

As he headed for the stainless steel refrigerator, Alexa pushed back her chair. "I'll help."

"I've got it," he told her. If he had his way and she became his mate, she'd never have to cook again.

The smell of frying bacon soon filled the air. J.J. turned the slices and scrambled eggs. The aroma did not make him hungry, it only infuriated him. Why hadn't Daniel fed Alexa?

When the food was ready, he doled it out in even portions.

As expected, both Darius and Aiden ate little, made excuses and left the kitchen. J.J. eyed his full plate and the males' and spoke in Spanish. "Guess I wasn't as hungry as I thought. Hate to see this good cooking go to waste."

He stabbed at an egg with a rueful look. "Even if I did burn it a bit."

J.J. scraped all the food onto Alexa's plate. She looked up, her eyes shiny. "Thanks. I know what you're doing. I was the only hungry one."

"When was the last time you had a square meal?" he asked gently.

"Oh, maybe a couple of days ago." She glanced down with a wry smile. "No big deal. I certainly can lose a few pounds."

"You're perfect for a female, maybe a little too thin. You need to eat." J.J. headed for the counter, and refilled her coffee mug. "Daniel doesn't have enough food on the ranch?"

The big fucker's belly certainly indicated he wasn't starving.

Alexa patted her mouth with a paper napkin. "He's rationed our food allowance until I can pay off the loan. My dad is pretty weak and sick, so I've given him my portion."

Tension shot through J.J.'s muscles. He balled his fists. Daniel was a bastard and Alexa needed to leave that pack before things got worse. Had he known Daniel was withholding food from Alexa and her family, he'd have thought twice about hurling him toward financial ruin.

After she finished, J.J. escorted her out of the lodge. On the wide porch, he hooked his thumbs into his belt and stared at the bright blue Montana sky.

"Sun's not setting for a while yet. You've got time before you have to head home. Let's go for a ride by the river. But my truck is parked at the barn."

Alexa gave her first real smile of the day and his heart pounded harder. "We can take mine. Well, it's not mine, but belongs to the pack."

When they reached the pickup, he tugged at the passenger door.

"It sticks a little. I've been meaning to oil it, but got too busy," she told him.

J.J. pulled harder and the door creaked open with a protesting groan. He helped her into the truck, closed the door and walked around the front. Rust covered the truck's grate and the bumper was missing. As he sat in the driver's seat, he shifted his weight to avoid a broken spring. When he turned the key in the ignition, the motor coughed like a dying bull.

J.J. glanced at Alexa, who flushed. "Daniel says he'll buy us a new truck soon."

Right. When cows learned to fly.

"I don't believe him, because Daniel is a liar. Like all alphas, he is power hungry and manipulative." She gave a tiny sigh as she opened the glove compartment and stuffed the check inside. "Soon as I'm done with this, I'm free of all alphas."

Can you set aside your hatred for me to become my mate? Gods, he wanted to howl. Or bang his head against the door in frustration.

She gave him a shy smile that tugged at his heart. "Thanks for staying with me. But I don't want to get you in trouble if you have to return to Colorado."

The only trouble I'll have is if I stutter my full name. J.J. shrugged. "My schedule is flexible."

Alarm filled him as he put the truck into drive and tested the brakes. He stopped. Barely. "This is your ranch's only vehicle?"

"Only one he loans out for errands."

And he lets his pack females drive this deathtrap while he drives a Jag? J.J. squelched his anger. As he drove to the dirt road leading to the barn, he stole a glance at his future mate. He decided to speak in English. Hell, around Alexa he could handle English without stammering. Maybe.

J.J. dragged in a deep, calming breath and spoke slowly. "Those muffins you made last month were delicious. You sure are a great baker."

Her smile softened her expression and chased away

the dark shadows beneath her huge blue eyes. "Thanks. I learned from my mother. She's the best. She had to be, cooking for all eight of us in the city."

"What city?"

"San Diego. I used to live there with my family." Alexa regarded him with a curious look. "And you? Do you miss living in Mexico, J.J.? How did you get that nickname? It's very American."

"It's short for Javier Juan, the name my mother gave me." He cleared his throat and spoke slower to control his stutter. "I never lived in Mexico. I was born in California. My father was American, my mother was Mexican."

Back in childhood, he'd been known as Javier Juan Garcia Taylor. He'd called himself J.J. to blend into the Anglo world. Later, determined to make his fortune, he'd dropped the Garcia and changed his name to Jeremiah Jackson to fit into the corporate world.

"You must have gotten those blue eyes from your father. And your dark hair from your mother. Are your parents still alive?"

"My mama is," he said vaguely. "She's in Mexico with my grandparents."

"You must miss them."

"Yes, but I have my own pack now. Pack is everything."

"No, it's not." Alexa set her jaw. "Packs are overrated. Living under the thumb of an alpha? No thanks. I went to college to get a business degree and make my life into a success to support my family, not get stuck with a lousy leader like Daniel."

"Daniel is a poor example of an alpha."

"Taylor is probably worse."

23

"Why do you hate Jeremiah Taylor so much?" I'm really not a bad guy. Well, when I'm not taking my revenge on assholes who tormented me...

"From what I've heard, he's arrogant, snooty and insensitive. I Googled him."

J.J.'s heart stilled. "See any photos?"

She frowned. "A couple. They were grainy pictures. Dark hair, hard to tell his features. The photos were shot from a distance when he was at a party."

Good.

"You must be so miserable, belonging to his pack and working for him," she added.

He bristled. "He's a decent guy."

"If he were decent, he wouldn't be purchasing my body. I'm afraid he's going to be a very crude and hasty lover."

J.J. controlled his urge to stop the truck, pull her into his arms and demonstrate exactly what kind of lover he was.

"Why do you think that?"

"The gossips say he likes one-night stands. And he doesn't engage women in conversation."

True, because he doesn't want to stammer like a fool.

When he'd formed his pack, he'd cultivated a reputation as an aloof, firm alpha. Because he wasn't a pedigreed alpha like Aiden Mitchell, he'd fought hard to establish himself as a tough SOB. Now that rep was trouble because Alexa Grant thought he was an arrogant, rich hard-ass.

At the barn, J.J. parked and they went into the building. The familiar smell of hay and horses proved soothing, cut with Alexa's delicate scent of female and flowers. He chose a sweet-tempered mare for her, and a gelding for himself.

They rode to the river, then dismounted, letting the horses crop the grass. Alexa gazed around the thicket of woods and the churning river. "I can't stand my life," she said as she stared into the frothing water.

He reached for her, wanting to promise the moon and the stars, but she ducked away. Alexa sat on the grassy riverbank and tugged off her boots and socks.

Her socks had holes in them.

And then she removed her shirt, and tugged off her jeans, standing before him in bra and panties. His jaw dropped.

Pink polka dots.

Her breasts nearly spilled out of the pink-polka dotted bra. Her hips were wide in the matching panties, and her waist had a gentle slope. He stared, his dick instantly hard.

"Yee haw!" She jumped into the water.

Alexa bobbed up in the water, flinging back her hair. "Damn, that's cold! You coming in?"

Oh hell yeah. He sat, tugged off his boots and then stripped to his black boxers. She treaded water and watched him with wide eyes.

J.J. jumped in and howled as the icy stream hit his skin. "Yeesh!"

He swam over to Alexa. "Current's wicked. You okay?"

She stood up, rising from the water like a dark-haired goddess. Her nipples poked through the bra's silk and his body forgot about the cold. "Not that deep. See?"

He laughed. "You're a vixen, Alexa Grant."

25

"Wolf. Not a vixen."

As she splashed him, J.J. pulled her into his arms and kissed her. Alexa closed her eyes. Her mouth tasted like bacon and honey. He expertly nibbled at her lower lip, coaxing her to open to him. As she did, he slid his tongue past her lips. Alexa gave a little moan, the sound going straight to his throbbing groin.

When they broke apart, her gaze turned troubled. He touched her cheek, hating to see her upset. "What's wrong?"

"I'm sorry. I want you, but can't do this. I have to remain pure for Jeremiah Taylor."

"Run away with me."

"I can't. I have to go through with this and give Taylor my virginity."

J.J. kissed her forehead. "Don't worry, darling. These things have a way of working themselves out. And soon, you'll be free of Daniel."

Tell her now. Tell her how you care and who you are.

"I wish you could be my first lover," she whispered.

Alexa pushed a hand through her wet hair and glanced to the right. He froze, remembering the same gesture from Selena. The whispered words of affection…and then standing in the barn, shivering and naked…

Alexa belonged to the same pack that had caused his total humiliation.

She pulled away and swam in strong strokes to the riverbank. As she climbed out, he watched the fabric pulled tight against her big, beautiful bottom. Man, he adored her ass.

He thought about taking her in the traditional mating

position. His hands on those wide hips as she knelt before him. His cock driving deep inside her to claim her in the flesh.

No other male would touch her, ever, he silently vowed. He was not letting her go. But he needed Alexa to see Jeremiah Taylor wasn't the bastard she thought. He had seven days to win her over, and prove he'd be a worthy mate. Seven days to make sure Alexa and Daniel didn't find out his real identity, because if she was working with Daniel, Daniel would love to screw him over.

Until Alexa was free of Daniel's pack, he couldn't fully trust her.

Because he'd sworn long ago on that cold November night, to never trust a woman from Daniel North's pack again.

CHAPTER 2

48 hours later…

Keeping a white-knuckled grip on the leather steering wheel of the blue Mustang convertible, Alexa glowered at the windshield. The V6 engine purred as the car ate up the miles. She cruised along the country road leading to the Double B ranch in Durango and the male who would callously take her innocence.

No matter how brutal a lover Jeremiah Taylor proved to be, she must go through with this.

Alexa pressed harder on the gas pedal, passing sedans and vans filled with Skins. Her raffia cowboy hat with the embroidered band was new, as were her turquoise Western boots, embroidered blue jeans and faux Western shirt with pink rhinestone butterflies. The outfit was hand-selected to annoy the thrifty Taylor. It was said he hated flashy women.

Her GPS bleated out instructions and she dutifully turned onto the dirt road beneath a sign reading "Double B Ranch." Alexa glanced down at her breasts. No way she'd fit in here. She was a double D, not a B cup.

Acres of green grass flanked her as she drove down the dirt road. Pretty, but no match for the rugged mountains of Montana she'd left behind.

Out of the corner of her eye she saw a horse and rider trotting toward her from the pasture. They were too close. Gonna collide! Alexa slammed on the brakes, but the horse galloped to the road's other side and the cowboy jerked his mount to a dead halt.

Her stomach gave a sickening twist. She switched off the ignition with a shaky hand.

The cowboy guided his mount over to her door and leaned over the saddle horn. A tan Stetson hid his face. Alexa glared at him. "You could have killed yourself."

He laughed, a full-bodied, deep drawl. Then he pushed his hat back on his head. His intense blue gaze, as bright as the Colorado skies, held hers.

"J.J!" She put a hand to her chest. "Damn, you scared me."

Her heart pounded faster as he dismounted and let the reins trail. J.J. stood more than six feet tall, with a lean, muscled body. Faded blue jeans covered his long legs and he wore a blue long-sleeved chambray work shirt. His feet were stuffed into a pair of scuffed Western boots. His gaze was deep and blue as a western sky in winter, and his tanned, lean features and mop of jet black curls hinted of mixed Hispanic blood.

J.J. was a sweetheart. Why he belonged to a pack ruled by an alpha as smug and arrogant as Jeremiah Taylor made no sense. Alexa got out and slammed the car door.

He gave a low bow and spoke in English. "Miss Alexa Grant. Welcome to the Double B."

Her mouth quirked in a smile. "Thanks. Nearly

29

running into a car, is that the way you greet all the guests?"

"Usually we pick them up at the La Plata airport. Unless they hire a rental car in Denver and don't have the courtesy to let us know they've decided to drive on their own instead of fly here."

Alexa shrugged. "I didn't have the number."

J.J. reached into the pocket of his work shirt, and then took her right hand. His hand was warm and rough. Not the hands of a lazy lout like his boss, who let his pack do all the work, but a rugged cowboy who got up close and personal with the land. A shiver skated down her palm as she caught the aroma of his scent. Pure Lupine male, mixed with leather.

Turning over her hand, he penned something on her palm. J.J. replaced the pen and grinned, his teeth white against the tanned darkness of his handsome face.

"Now you have no excuses. Next time, call."

"Now that I have your number, I will." She gazed at the two-story house and the nearby red barn. "Where should I park? I want to meet His Highness and get introductions over with."

She sounded like a prisoner headed to her execution. Alexa felt as depressed as one.

J.J. quirked an eyebrow and rubbed his clean-shaven chin. "His Highness?"

"Isn't that what you call your alpha? Or is it His High Anus?"

He gave another quick, wide grin. "Jeremiah would do. I'll meet you at the main house. Go down the gravel drive to the building on the left."

He mounted and she watched him, admiring how his tight jeans stretched over his very fine butt. Alexa sighed and climbed back into the car and drove to the main house.

She waited for J.J. to arrive and tie his horse a hitching post set before the two-story white building. He snagged her suitcase as she popped the trunk.

He pointed out the flat meadows banked by the Animas River. "The Double B specializes in providing breeding stock and thoroughbreds. There's trail rides for Skins in the summer and fall that help fund the pack's other needs, like education for the young. Recently we bought a herd of goats and started making our own organic cheese. Tourists wandering through Durango in the summer love that stuff. We even have our own beehives and make honey."

J.J.'s obvious enthusiasm for the ranch loosened the tight knot in her stomach. "At least your alpha has an eye for business."

"No reason a good alpha will let his pack starve or a business go belly up." J.J. stroked a finger across his chin. "If one business fails, you start another. Pack comes first. Always provide for pack, that's what Taylor says."

"You sound like Taylor's number one cheerleader. Did he send you to convince me how wonderful he is?"

No matter, she wasn't buying it.

"He's not bad. Give him a chance."

"I don't have a choice, do I?"

His gaze turned intense. "There's always choices. No one should force anyone into anything they don't want. 'Specially a p—" J.J. closed his eyes and inhaled deeply through his nose.

"J.J.? Are you okay?"

"Fine." He hissed out a breath, opened his eyes and

31

said in Spanish. "A pretty Lupine like you. Don't let anyone dictate your life."

A lump clogged her throat again. She replied in the same language. "Would love that, except to consummate this arrangement, I have to go along for the ride."

"And what kind of ride are you expecting, *cariño*?"

Alexa gave him a sideways look. With his tall, athletic body, lazy grace and easy manner, J.J. made her feel all cranked up and hot. More hot than she'd ever become with her future one-night stand.

"Not a very pleasant one. But it's only for one night," she told him, gazing around the grounds.

The ranch was bisected by the fast-moving river, with a few bridges built across. Acres of green meadow stretched far as she could see. Horses grazed in a nearby pasture, and next to the red barn was a small holding pen where fat goats nosed in the dirt for food.

The Double B held an undertone of wildness. Maybe it was the stretch of pine and aspen trees across the river marching up the cliffs where a wolf could roam wild and catch prey. Or the rugged cowhand standing by her.

She smiled at him and switched back to English. "Your boss should have named it the Wild Wolf Ranch. It's very freeing, all this space."

J.J.'s mouth quirked in a grin. "It's a good place to live. You'll see."

The deep timbre of his gravelly voice sent shivers shooting down her spine. J.J. had a seductive voice, a baritone that could seduce the clothing off a woman. And his big, work-roughened hands....

Putting a hand at the small of her back, J.J. escorted

her to the wide steps of the lodge. "This is where Taylor bunks. His office is on the second floor, bedroom down the hallway."

Curious, she gazed around the deserted yard. "Where is everyone?"

"Most of the hands are helping a neighbor for a few days. You have a choice. You can bunk at the guest house where we let tourists stay. Or you can sleep here, where Taylor lives. He's got lots of rooms."

A bed of nails would feel more comfortable than a room close to Jeremiah Taylor.

"I'll take the guest house. And where are you staying?"

A line dented between his black brows and he gave her an odd, questioning look. Then he pointed to a building closer to the river. "The guest house. Taylor wants me to make sure you don't need anything."

He dumped her suitcase and carry-on into a golf cart and they drove down a paved pathway to a large adobe building by the river.

J.J. parked the cart and snagged her suitcase and carry-on and lugged them inside. There was a great room with a desk made from birch, a stone fireplace and a staircase leading to the second floor. He led her down a narrow hallway to a door marked with a brass plate reading "Number Five."

"During the summer, he rents out rooms to other Lupines wanting a real ranch experience," he explained.

"For money. That's all that Taylor cares about."

He shook his head. "An alpha must do whatever he can to tend to his pack. And it's not all about the money."

"You'll never convince me."

33

The cowboy tipped back his hat and his gaze grew sharp. "You are a stubborn little Lupine. You've already judged him and you haven't even met him."

"I'll meet him soon enough." Alexa's palms grew clammy.

He spoke in rapid Spanish. "Alexa, I need to level with you. Jeremiah Jackson Taylor is not what you think."

She stared at him, her heart racing. "Dear goddess, is he deformed? Incapable of performing?"

His mouth twitched in apparent amusement. "No. But if I told you he was a normal, ordinary Lupine who desires you, who wanted to help you out and has only your best interests at heart, would it change your mind about him?"

"No. He'd have to prove it." She glanced down the hallway, wondering if the mysterious billionaire was lurking nearby. "Where is he?"

"Taylor is very reclusive. He asked me to take over, show you around the ranch and how it works."

"How soon will I meet him? A day? Two? Five years? A century?"

He gave her a funny look and said, "At the end of the seven days."

Relief filled her. A reprieve. Maybe if she were lucky, they'd do the deed in the dark and she'd never see his face.

He explained the code to open the guest house's front door and the guest room, then he opened the door to her room. "After you."

The room was large, comfortable and had a fireplace and a king bed. French doors led to a porch overlooking the river. "This is very nice."

"It's small compared to the main house. You may be more comfortable there."

She didn't want to get anywhere near Jeremiah Jackson Taylor's bedroom and get her scent all over his living quarters. Not until she sprayed herself with Eau de Skunk first. "I'll stay here."

J.J. rolled her suitcase over to the closet. He tipped his hat back. "Anything I can get you? I have work, but I'll be back before dinner. Mini fridge is stocked with soft drinks and water, and there's chilled Chardonnay in the living room fridge. We serve it to guests at five o'clock."

"I don't drink."

"It's very good wine. We serve it to all the guests."

Now it was her turn to raise her brows. "Part of the guest services your ranch offers to a guest doomed to sleep with the alpha?"

He didn't even blink. "Goes with our in-room service of cleaning rhinestones. Though it might take a few days to shine up those puppies." He nodded at the butterflies on her chest. "Got a whole field of butterflies there."

"Yes, obnoxious, isn't it?"

"I like butterflies." He gave a wide grin.

She touched a rhinestone. "I heard Jeremiah Taylor doesn't like glitz. Only reason I bought this ridiculous outfit. This isn't the real me. I like clothing that doesn't sparkle in the sun."

J.J. remained silent, watching her.

"I told my parents I was going away for a few days to make some money." She shook her head. "I couldn't bear telling them how I was doing it. I told them I'd be fine. But even though he assured me all would work out, I could see it in my dad's eyes. Nothing is

35

going to be fine until we can leave Daniel's control."

"He doesn't want you to worry," he said gently.

She gave a little sigh. "It's my fault for believing Daniel's promises. I knew Dad needed a good pack after his health started failing and Daniel told us we'd be treated like family."

J.J.'s mouth compressed. "That's not a lie. Daniel treats his family like dirt."

"Well, he treats his pack worse. I was desperate to get Dad settled, so I could get on with my life. We stayed with Daniel for an introductory period of 30 days and everything was wonderful. I signed a blood contract, binding us to Daniel as our alpha. And then the mask fell off and we saw the real Daniel."

She frowned. "It was really weird. He was nice and friendly when we first met, and then turned completely opposite, as if he were two different people. Every once in a rare while, he treats us decently."

J.J.'s broad shoulders tensed. "Once in a while, as if he's struggling with the idea?"

"Yeah. I once stumbled upon him in private, crying as if he were in pain. When I asked if I could do anything, he turned into a bastard again. It got worse. Never enough food to eat, and then he pressured my mother to work for him and even my younger siblings. I only got to escape when I told him I could help him if I went to college."

"And then he ensnared you further by loaning you the money."

Alexa hugged herself. "Ever feel like your life is spinning out of control and you're helpless to stop it? You have no power and you'd give anything to escape your life?"

"I've been there. Why did Daniel throw you to the ground at Aiden's ranch?"

Humiliation crawled over her. "He wanted to accompany me upstairs to watch me sign the papers. He wanted to rub it in that I was selling my innocence, the only thing that is mine. He said I'd probably cry." Alexa ran a hand through her hair and glanced away, not wanting to meet his gaze because she wanted more than anything for J.J. to respect her.

J.J. said nothing, only waited for her to continue.

"I told him to go home and wait for his damn money and I'd never cry. No one ever sees me cry."

"Daniel's a cruel alpha. You deserve better."

"I doubt Taylor will be better. I'm an idiot for trapping myself in this mess. Why did I ever trust Daniel? I know I can't trust Taylor. What if he decides to keep me here longer than the seven days? I have to return to my family. They need me. I don't know how much more my dad can take."

"Hey. Don't give up so easily. It's going to be okay." J.J. leaned close and cupped her cheek, his calloused thumb rubbing over her skin. It felt so good to have a man touch her with tenderness. Alexa leaned toward him.

His mouth was warm and firm as he kissed her, a brief brush against her lips. Alexa sighed and then he backed off. "Shouldn't have done that."

Kiss me again, please. Kiss me again and shut away the world and all its reality. But she was promised to another male's bed.

J.J. touched her cheek, his touch making her shiver. Oh why couldn't she lose her virginity to him instead of Jeremiah Taylor?

37

"Call me if you need anything."

When he left, she unpacked her clothing and put it away. Lastly, she removed her most precious talisman—a small cheerful gnome statue her best friend Jessica had given her in college. The gnome, which she'd dubbed Herman, was a good luck charm and went everywhere with her.

Alexa stroked Herman's faded red cap. "I hope you do bring good luck, because I sure could use it this week."

She set the gnome on the fireplace mantel, flopped onto the bed and stared at the popcorn ceiling. Alexa bit her lip, fighting the lump of emotion clogging her throat. Auctioning off her virginity to a total stranger had been the last resort. But at least her family would remain safe.

She fished out her phone and texted Molly and Jessica, her best friends. The three female Lupines called themselves the Chub Club after banding together during their freshman year at the University of Florida. A snotty sorority president had mocked them during rush week, calling them fat. In turn, Jessica dumped a laxative mixture into the president's beer during a party. They all watched in great satisfaction as the sorority president farted so much everyone left the room.

I'm here. Not met Taylor yet. J.J. showed me around the ranch. Cute! Makes my blood howl. Wish I had my Spanx to tame my big butt, Alexa wrote.

Forget the Spanx. Male Lupines like curves, Jessica texted back.

U gonna b ok? Molly texted.

Sure. One night and then it's over. Alexa wished she could believe it.

Tell Taylor to go blow. Tell me more about what happened with J.J. Jessica texted.

Went skinny dipping in river w him at the Mitchell Ranch.

Alexa! Molly texted.

OMG! Word! Jessica texted.

Word. Well, I wore bra and panties. He wore boxers...icy water but no shrinkage!!!

OMG. Maybe you should do him instead of that uncaring bastard Taylor, Jessica texted.

I wish. But a deal is a deal. Alexa felt miserable. She missed her friends and felt so alone and alienated. Molly lived in Florida and Jess had moved back to Michigan after graduation.

Love u guys. C u.

Alexa signed off, wishing her first lover could be someone as gentle and sexy as J.J. But she had signed the papers and would never risk Taylor demanding his money back.

J.J. made her feel all tingly and aware. Her wolf wanted to howl with desire when she saw him.

How ironic she'd saved herself for the right male, never sleeping with anyone in college so she could be a virgin when she met her mate. Now at 23, she stood to lose her innocence to an uncaring, callous man who bought her like he bought stocks and bonds.

Alexa stared at the ceiling, dreading the night she would give herself to Taylor.

And she wasn't certain that Daniel wouldn't renege on his promise once he received the money. Daniel didn't have to sign anything. She had to rely on his verbal promise.

I'll find a way to be free of that asshole. Somehow.

J.J. stomped dust off his boots as he headed into the main house. He hated lying. It grated against his whole being. But he didn't trust Alexa yet with his deepest secret.

What if Daniel discovered his real identity? No, it wasn't time, not yet.

Running up the stairs to his second floor office, he ruminated over the blizzard of paperwork awaiting him. Most of his cowboys were away, but a few were still needed to run the ranch.

The hard-working *vaqueros* he'd taken into his pack knew him as J.J. No formalities. They were not blood, but he felt closer to them than family.

Removing his Stetson, he placed it on the hat rack just inside the door. J.J. sat in the leather desk chair and stared at his computer screen. Everything in the office was high tech and expensive, contrasting to the old-fashioned farmhouse.

He wanted the office to look sleek and important. Impressive and wealthy. After all, he bought and traded stocks in here, not livestock. But he was uncomfortably aware that the décor reflected an old insecurity.

You're 35 years old and part of you, deep inside, is still that dirt poor pup.

J.J. thought of Alexa trapped in Daniel's pack. Gods, he knew the helplessness, the bitter frustration of having no control over one's life. If she truly was trapped and wasn't lying about Daniel. But that glance away, like Selena had done, it was usually a sign of someone lying…

No one ever sees me cry, Alexa had told him.

40

He opened a desk drawer and removed a faded photo. A family photo, two years after their arrival at his uncle's house.

At his Cousin Daniel's house.

Images from the past clicked through his mind like a slideshow. J.J. had been nine years old and hungry. His father had lost everything. They had no money. No power. No pack. The once proud alpha begged his brother-in-law for a place to live because he didn't want his only offspring and mate living in the woods.

J.J. and Daniel were best buddies, only two years apart. He loved living in his uncle's pack. He and Daniel played in his cousin's tree house deep in the dark woods. They hunted frogs together in the pond, played stickball and were inseparable. When they'd found an old tire in the woods, Daniel had tied it to a rope on tree and J.J. had spent many happy hours, swinging from the tire as Daniel pushed him.

And then two years later, shortly after his first shift into wolf, Daniel changed. The abrupt change in personality bewildered J.J. as Daniel turned mean and nasty. He began mocking J.J., calling him a half-breed dirty Mexican. Made fun of him for being poor.

Like Alexa, he'd once chanced upon Daniel crying alone. His cousin had looked up at him with big, woebegone eyes and pleaded, "Help me."

Then his features seemed to ripple, and J.J. thought it was a trick of sunlight. Because after that, Daniel turned even more cruel.

J.J. had one treasured possession, Georgie, his stuffed teddy bear. A day after the crying incident, Daniel snatched Georgie. Later, J.J. found Georgie in the trash, his arms and legs ripped off, one eye missing.

41

J.J. had secretly buried him in the woods, tears running down his cheeks. He'd wiped away the tears with a dingy shirt sleeve.

Like Alexa, no one ever saw him cry, either.

He pulled himself away from the memory, tucked the photo back inside the drawer and powered up the computer. But the entire time he worked, he couldn't forget the misery on Alexa's face.

He knew how she felt, powerless and alone. Life wasn't fair. But he'd do everything to ensure she never wanted again.

If only he could trust her.

CHAPTER 3

Happy hour at a ranch where she never expected to be happy.

At five, Alexa went into the living room and found the wine, as J.J. had promised. After seeing too many drunk students in college, she'd shied away from liquor, but maybe she should start drinking now. It could help dull her senses when she went to Taylor's bed. She poured herself a glass.

Cool air caressed her cheeks as she carried the wine and bottle to the back porch. Pink streaked the blue sky as the sun began to set. Alexa sat at a glass-topped table, set down the bottle and sipped the wine.

Wow. She liked the flavor, picking up hints of tangy oak and citrus. She studied the distant mountains streaked with red striated rock, the ribbon of river bisecting the ranch. So peaceful and quiet.

Didn't matter.

She wasn't staying longer than the week.

Why did Jeremiah Taylor want her? It made no sense. When she'd questioned Aiden Mitchell, he'd said Taylor had seen her at an event she'd catered. He'd been smitten with her tarts. Or maybe it was her tits. She wasn't certain, as Aiden had mumbled.

Swirling the clear white liquid in her glass, she took a long pull. Excellent. Alexa drank some more.

"Mind if I join you?" a deep voice drawled.

Her heart skipped a beat as she looked up to see J.J.'s Stetson pulled low on his forehead, blue jeans faded, but clean. A blue chambray work shirt outlined his leanly muscled body. An empty wineglass dangled incongruously from one calloused, bronzed hand.

Her heart raced and her body felt tight with longing. The wolf was so damn hot.

Alexa gestured to an empty chair. "Want some wine?"

He helped himself and studied her with that keen, assessing look. "I thought you didn't drink."

"Now's a good time to start." She swirled the liquid in her glass.

A planter filled with bright red geraniums sat on the deck. The cool river breeze teased her hair as she watched horses crop grass in the nearby pasture. The bucolic, peaceful setting should have soothed her anxiety, but Alexa could only think of the fate awaiting her in Jeremiah Jackson Taylor's bed.

A shudder of revulsion raced down her spine as she imagined Taylor's hands, his body rudely penetrating hers without gentleness or consideration. Certainly not love.

J.J. clinked glasses with her. "To your future."

The delicious wine turned sour in her mouth. "I'd rather drink to something more positive. Like nuclear war."

He considered. "How about drinking to good times?"

Much better. She clinked glasses with him again.

"And great sex."

Alexa nearly choked on her sip of wine. She recovered and saw him watching her with his hooded gaze. "That's an odd toast."

He shrugged. "Why? I'm a guy. I think of sex all the time. You're a young, healthy Lupine. We're a sensual people. Haven't you ever wondered what great sex would be like?"

"I don't have a good imagination."

But that was a lie, for she had wondered, and felt wistful that her body would be turned over to an uncaring, arrogant alpha who only wanted her for his own purposes—the cheap thrill of taking her high-priced virginity. "Would you like me to illustrate for you?"

A teasing look entered his gaze. Despite the chilly river breeze, Alexa felt hot all over. "Only if you use my body as your canvas."

Did she actually say that? A furious blush heated her face, but J.J. only threw back his head and laughed. He had a wonderful laugh, deep and relaxed.

"Might be better to tell you in Spanish."

"Why not English?"

He considered. "Sounds more romantic in Spanish."

"I could do with a little romance." She sighed deeply. "Instead I'll be handed over to an arrogant male who will climb on top of me, do the deed and think only of himself. Not exactly how I wanted to experience sex for the first time."

Oops. The wine made her careless.

But he only regarded her with his steady gaze. "The first time a woman makes love can be painful, but also

45

filled with pleasure if you have the right partner."

Such intensity in his eyes, as if he wanted to be that special someone who made love to her for the very first time. Alexa envisioned J.J. naked, all those wiry muscles, mounting her as she lay naked in bed. His hard male body covering her as he looked down with passion blazing in his intense gaze...

She felt so warm and relaxed. No, hot and wet. Wet between the legs. Oh, she'd had those feelings before, but not cranked up like this, as if someone had jerked her internal thermostat to flaming hot.

Alexa stole glances at J.J., who stretched out his long legs. Tight jeans hugged his lean, muscular thighs. And that ass, very fine indeed.

"Eres muy simpatico. Que lindo culo tienes," she murmured.

He raised a dark brow. "Thanks for the compliment. I've never thought of myself as cute, or possessing a nice ass, but I appreciate your assessment."

She'd forgotten he spoke fluent Spanish. Alexa tried to gather her scrambled brain cells, but it felt like herding a litter of naughty puppies. Spanish, Spanish...

"How did you learn Spanish?"

J.J. set his glass down on the glass tabletop. "My mother."

"How many siblings?"

"Just me."

"Must have been lonely." She studied his lean, handsome face. "And you grew up here in Colorado? Did you belong to a pack?"

He picked up his wine glass again and drank. "My father was an alpha who lost everything. We had to live with his sister and her husband and pack. It was hell on my dad, Uncle Dickhead rubbing it in that my father had failed. He killed himself two years after we moved."

Stunned, she turned to him. His mouth flattened and he stared at the mountains. Alexa gently touched his shirt sleeve. "I'm so sorry, J.J."

He gave a brusque nod.

"Did your mother leave your uncle's pack after you lost your father? It must have been so difficult for her to stay there."

"She was sad and lonely after Dad died and returned to Mexico to find her family's pack."

"You didn't go?"

"I was an honor student at the local Skin school. My mama said if I went with her, I'd never achieve my full potential. She wanted me to be someone."

Sympathy filled her. "I'm sure she would be proud. Do you ever get to see her?"

"Sometimes. Not enough." A wistful smile touched his full mouth.

Alexa couldn't imagine being without her family. Her close-knit family was the only reason she'd returned home after college. She'd do anything to keep them all together.

"We went to Daniel's pack because we were homeless after my dad fell ill. Daniel said if we joined his pack, he'd take care of us. I was required to sign a blood oath of loyalty. You know the oath you can't break according to Lupine law and you need the alpha's permission to cancel it?"

He nodded.

"Daniel's controlled our lives ever since. He refuses to let my family leave his pack."

47

"Because Daniel is an SOB who enjoys tormenting others, especially those who can't fight back."

Alexa watched J.J. pour more wine into her glass. She shouldn't drink so much, but this feeling was so delicious and warm, she wanted to hold onto it a while longer.

Mexico. The country kept dancing about in her head. Odd. The wine had muddied her thoughts and she couldn't think straight. "How did you meet Jeremiah?"

He gave her an odd look. "I got to know Jeremiah after I realized I'd never be taken for anything but a half-breed Mexican. If you want to get anywhere in the Skin world, you need connections. I had none."

Alexa sensed the real male lay hidden beneath the surface, and what she'd seen was a mere ripple in the waters.

"Connections aren't as important as family. Nothing, not even money, is as important as family."

"Without money, you can't help your family," he pointed out.

True enough. Alexa pushed aside the depressing thought and studied J.J. Wineglass dangling from one hand, he casually crossed his long legs at the ankles.

"You're very nice to be around. Not uptight like those in my pack. Daniel is so wound up—he acts like someone superglued his butt cheeks together."

Alexa slapped a hand over her mouth, but J.J. laughed. "It's okay, Alexa. You're permitted to mock the alpha here. You're among friends."

It felt good to relax and not worry that Daniel was eavesdropping. "I don't have friends back home. Everyone's too afraid to have any kind of relationship."

"He's that controlling?"

Nodding, she studied her glass. "I work in the accounting office, help organize the financial spreadsheets. If I'm five minutes late to work, Daniel doesn't pay me for half a day. Excuses don't matter. I've been late quite a few times this year because Mom needs my help with Dad and my brothers and sisters in the morning."

She leaned forward, somehow wanting to make this compassionate Lupine understand what drove her to sell her body. "I hired myself out as a cook at times to other packs to bring in extra income. Daniel allowed it because it enhanced his reputation; having a pack member who was an excellent cook. But that didn't help. Right now I owe Daniel so much money I'll never be able to pay him back—unless I do something crazy, like sell my body for half a million dollars. I know what that makes me look like...but I'm not that way. I just want to take my family out of there, to a place where they can feel safe and comfortable, not with constant threats hanging over their heads."

"Daniel is an ass." A low growl rumbled in J.J.'s throat.

"A dangerous one." The wine had loosened her tongue. But for too long she'd suppressed her anger, fearing retribution against her father. "If Daniel wanted to evict us, he could. He has absolute power. That's why I despise Jeremiah Taylor. Rich Lupines like him don't care about others. My family and I have lived with Daniel for five years and Monday morning after I sleep with Taylor, we're leaving."

J.J.'s blue gaze sharpened as he studied her. "You're certain it's worth sleeping with Taylor, since you hate him that much?"

Her stomach knotted. Alexa shook her head. "A contract is a contract and it's only for one night."

"You make it sound like you're going to a torture chamber and not Jeremiah's bed. Sex isn't that bad, Alexa."

"It is when you've saved yourself for someone special." She'd wanted her first time to be sex with someone she loved. What a joke. Love was an overrated idea among a species known for their powerful sensuality. Why did she cling to such silly, old-fashioned ideals?

J.J. gave her an intent look. "Jeremiah Taylor is a decent Lupine. Trust me on this."

But I'll never love him. I can never love someone like him because he's just a figurehead and a bully. I refuse to worship a master, a god who can strike you down on a whim, with a thunderbolt. I don't know him, but I know you, and damn, I could fall in love with you.

I think I already am falling...

"I think you're pretty decent yourself," she told him softly.

Alexa leaned over and kissed his cheek, tasting the slight stubble of his night beard. It was just a brush of her mouth against his skin, but it heated her blood. J.J. set down his wineglass on the table and his eyes darkened.

"Much as I'd like to explore where this is headed, you need dinner. I promised myself I'd feed you a lot while you're here."

I'd rather dine on you for dinner. That would be nice. You, naked with dinner spread over your torso.... me licking it off your body...

Nipples aching against the lace and satin bra, she

wanted to rub herself against J.J. Alexa felt swollen and wet between her legs.

His nostrils flared as if he'd caught the smell of her arousal. But he only murmured, "Dinner first, Miss Grant."

He pulled her upright and she nearly fell against him. His hand was warm and rugged, like the Lupine himself. His scent of leather was strong and intoxicating. What would it be like, making babies with him? Certainly the young would be adorable, fathered by J.J.

"I wish it was you, J.J. Only you. But I won't kiss you anymore. I don't want to get you into trouble with Jeremiah."

He gave her a funny look. "Oh, he won't mind."

Hooking an arm around her waist, he escorted her to the main house. Cicadas sang in the biting night air. She wasn't cold. A delicious heat spiraled through her at his nearness. The male was a furnace.

Sleeping with him in a big bed, while a frosty wind roared outside and a fire crackled in the hearth... now there was a fantasy she'd enjoy.

Maybe she could keep that image in her head when she had sex with Jeremiah Taylor.

He ushered her into the main house to a dining room bigger than her entire house. Sparkling silverware, linen napkins and a heavy gold brocade tablecloth covered a table long as a train. A chilled bottle of white wine sat in a sterling silver bucket stand. Soft light from a glittering chandelier glinted off the elegant white charger plates.

So much formality. Fit for a billionaire. Alexa thought about the scratched wood table in her family's postage-sized dining room. They'd bought it at Goodwill. Her family's furniture either came from Goodwill or garage sales.

J.J. slid out her chair and pushed it in, once she was seated. "Do you like the dining room?"

"It's got a quaint museum quality. Like the Smithsonian."

He crooked a grin. "Jeremiah entertains business clients here."

She rapped the table with her knuckles. "He must have plenty of clients, because this table is large enough to host all of Wall Street. When is the butler serving dinner? Or are there two butlers, one for each of us?"

J.J. uncorked the wine bottle. "No butler here, only the pack's cook and housekeeper. Jane's a terrific cook. And we're not eating alone. We'll be joined by Raphael, the ranch beta. I have a few things to go over with him."

"If he's the beta, what are you?"

"I keep things working around here." J.J. filled both their glasses.

How odd to sit here in jeans and T-shirt. Alexa glanced around, sweat beading her forehead. Such opulence. What if she used the wrong fork?

"Should I have dressed for dinner?"

A hank of black hair spilled over his forehead as he sat across from her. J.J. brushed it back with an impatient hand. "We aren't as formal as the furniture. Long as you come to the table wearing something, you'll do. No satin or lace required."

"My bra is satin and lace."

His gaze glittered hotly as he stared at her. "I've seen your underwear, Alexa. And unless you want me

52

to do what I did to you in the river when we were both wet, you'll keep your shirt on."

Her nipples tingled at the memory of his hot kisses, his hard mouth pressed against hers, his tongue thrusting deep. But she had to maintain distance from him because if she violated the contract, her family lost everything.

To distract herself, she gazed around at the room again. Maybe it was more White House than Smithsonian, come to think of it. "Very...overwhelming."

J.J.'s gaze turned hooded as he drank his wine. "Taylor believes in owning the best."

"Taylor sounds like a pompous ass," she said, sipping from her glass. Delicious, tangy and sweet.

"Stop judging him when you don't even know him. He's honest and decent."

"If he were an honest, decent male, why does he have a reputation as a callous jerk?"

Jaw tightening, J.J. shook his head. "He's a businessman. He's tough in business. You have to be, to make the numbers work. It isn't a charity. "

"I bet he's only hard in the boardroom, not the bedroom." Alexa bit her lip.

"He can be quite gentle in the bedroom." J.J. gave her that funny look again. "The ladies say he's a good lover, better than other alphas, like yours."

"Daniel isn't interested in women. I've never seen him take a mate, or even a lover. I think he's more interested in abusing his power than chasing after females."

The door to the dining room opened and a middle-aged woman in a navy blue dress and white apron

53

carried in a silver tray heaped with small appetizers. She gave Alexa a warm smile.

"Hi. I'm Jane, the ranch cook and housekeeper. Are you comfortable enough in the guest house? It tends to get drafty by the river. If you need more firewood, I'll have my mate, Emmanuel, come over and drop off a cord."

Alexa smiled. Jane had a motherly air. "It's perfect. I'm fine."

"Dinner will be ready in a few minutes," Jane said. "I made filet mignon, twice-baked potatoes and asparagus. Is that okay with you?"

She looked anxiously at Alexa.

"Filet of minion, that's what I call it. Sounds yummy. I adore grilled minion. Is yours cowhands who didn't get their work done?" Alexa grinned and Jane laughed at the joke.

J.J. chuckled and nodded at Jane.

"I've been fretting all day about what to serve. We sometimes make do with chili around here, but I want to make you feel comfortable," Jane told her.

Why was it so important to please her? Alexa pushed back a lock of hair. "I'm sure I'll love it. I'm not fussy. Chili is good, too."

"Alexa makes a mean Texas-style chili. She cooked last month for Aiden Mitchell's cowboys. Her chili put fur on their chests." J.J. winked at her and Alexa smiled at the compliment.

"I'm not a great cook, but I do okay. I've worked for a few packs in Montana and Colorado during the summer. So no worries, whatever you make will be terrific."

The female Lupine beamed at her. "Just as I thought. You'll do good."

"She'll do fine. Jane, serve the meal." J.J. gave an impatient glance at the housekeeper.

"What about…"

"If he can't be here on time, we're not waiting."

"Yes sir."

The housekeeper vanished into the kitchen.

"Yes sir? She acts as if you're in charge."

J.J. drummed his fingers on the table. "I run things around here. Jane's a wonderful housekeeper. Of course when Jeremiah chooses a mate, she worries about pleasing the new mistress."

"Is he going to shop around? He has enough money to purchase one. I hear QVC is starting to sell Lupine mates."

Swirling the wine in his glass, he leaned forward. "You have quite the mouth on you, Alexa. I may have to find a way of keeping you quiet."

"Duct tape works."

"So does a kiss."

She wanted him to kiss her again, wanted it badly, so badly she could taste his mouth against hers. Alexa scrubbed her lips with her index finger.

"I can't kiss you. I can't risk it."

"Because of Jeremiah?"

She nodded. "It must be nice to be a billionaire and not have to mate for money."

"When Jeremiah does settle down, it will be with the right woman, one he will care for and cherish the rest of his life," J.J. said quietly.

"Sounds romantic. I wish him luck." She stared at her wineglass, depressed all over again.

Jane served dinner and they began to eat. Alexa asked J.J. questions about the ranch.

A few minutes later, the front door opened and closed. J.J. looked up, his manner guarded. A tall man carrying a leather briefcase entered the dining room. A charcoal suit covered his muscled body and he had a solemn look in his black eyes. His hair was jet black too, the curls falling to his white starched collar. A neatly trimmed black beard and mustache framed a mouth almost too full and sensual for a male. His tanned skin hinted of a Mediterranean heritage. Alexa's heart dropped to her stomach.

He looked dangerous as a hungry wolf.

"Jeremiah Taylor," she whispered.

The stranger glanced at J.J. and his mouth quirked slightly. He set down the briefcase and nodded to her. "Miss Grant, welcome to the Double B Ranch. I am Raphael Amador, Mr. Taylor's assistant and his beta wolf."

"I thought you were Jeremiah Taylor." Confusion filled her. "You look like the photos I've seen."

He inclined his head again. "The press can be easily fooled. I've attended a few social events on Mr. Taylor's behalf, as he is disinclined to make public appearances."

As J.J. poured the beta a glass of wine, Raphael approached, picked up her hand and elegantly kissed it. He was quite handsome, but she felt no spark, no flare of chemistry. Not like she did when J.J. touched her.

She glanced up to see J.J.'s face tighten. Raphael gave an amused look and sat next to her. His scent was quite strong: the sharp bite of icy snow mixed with sandalwood. Not artificial, like cologne. And not leather and pure male like J.J.

Alexa's guard went up. If this man was Taylor's

beta, why did he have such a powerful scent? Usually only alpha males possessed that ability, mainly to attract females.

Raphael sat, unfolded his napkin, helped himself to beef and vegetables and began to eat.

"Rafe," J.J. said curtly. "Did you seal the deal?"

"They agreed to Mr. Taylor's terms." Raphael sipped his wine. "Of course, they were left with little choice."

"What deal?" Alexa asked.

"Purchase of Caballo Rojo, a champion racing stallion. Mr. Taylor wishes to put him to stud. The owners did not wish to part with him, but when Mr. Taylor wants something, he always obtains it."

So cold and heartless. "He buys horses like he purchases women."

Raphael turned his head and pinned his cold, dark gaze on her. "Mr. Taylor is a very sharp businessman. He has his reasons for what he chooses to do."

"Rafe, lay off," J.J. admonished in Spanish.

Raphael's mouth flattened, but he returned to his meal.

"So you understand Spanish. Do you speak it well?" she asked the taciturn Lupine.

"I lived in Mexico, princess." Raphael speared a piece of steak and ate it, but studied her as if she were a butterfly pinned to a specimen board.

"Alexa, would you care to go riding tomorrow morning?" J.J. asked.

"I don't ride."

A gleam ignited his gaze as he leaned over the table. "It would be my pleasure to teach you, *cariño.*"

Tension radiated from the man sitting beside her.

57

She wondered if Rafael was protective of his boss and didn't like the sexual byplay because she was marked for Jeremiah Taylor. Good.

"Maybe you can teach me other activities as well," she told J.J. "Ones that might come in useful Sunday night when I fulfill the terms of the contract in Mr. Taylor's bed."

Raphael choked on a sip of wine. He glared at J.J. and began speaking another language that sounded like Italian. She tried to follow the thread, but he spoke too fast. Then J.J. narrowed his gaze and switched back to English.

"Enough. We're being rude to Miss Grant."

Turning his full attention on her, J.J. asked about her college studies. When he discovered she enjoyed finance, they began a hearty discussion of the current market. Raphael sat silently, eating his meal and watching her.

Unease pricked her spine. The beta seemed far too interested. And why was he acting on behalf of Jeremiah Taylor in business deals?

Unless the man was Jeremiah Taylor and disguising himself. This stony man with the dark eyes? He seemed cold and remote and emitted little warmth, like a distant star. And he would be the one touching her naked body, his body sliding over hers, little care taken for her first time…

Alexa set down her fork, her stomach churning.

"Are you all right? You look very pale," J.J. observed.

"I don't feel well."

He rushed to her side, crouching down. "Rafe, get some cold water."

Raphael rose elegantly and headed for the kitchen.

J.J. put a hand to her forehead, his touch soothing. He had a compassionate manner. But she would not be sharing *his* bed Sunday night. "I know what's going on. I know the secret you're hiding."

He went very still, searching her face. "And?"

"It makes me sick. I don't know…" She swallowed hard against the bile rising in her throat. "I don't know if I can do this."

His touch felt soothing as he rubbed a thumb over her cheek. "It's not what you think. It's going to be okay. Trust me."

Raphael returned with a glass of water. Alexa grabbed it and chugged it down. She set down the glass and gave a wan smile. "It's been a long day. I should go to bed."

"Yes," Raphael murmured.

"To sleep," she added hastily.

"I'll escort you back." J.J. stood, but she waved him off. "Please. I can find my own way."

He studied her a long moment, giving her that same inscrutable look. "Jane," he called out. "Please walk Alexa back to the guest quarters."

The friendly housekeeper emerged, wiping her hands on the apron. "Of course. You okay honey?" She frowned at J.J. and Raphael. "I know these two can be overwhelming at times. And it's been a long day for you."

The motherly concern nearly broke Alexa. She fisted her hands. "Fine. Thank you for a terrific meal."

J.J. squeezed her hand. "Good night, Alexa. I'll see you tomorrow at breakfast."

She did not look back as they headed for the front

door, but she swore two pairs of male eyes were burning into her back.

And her instinct warned her that one set belonged to Jeremiah Taylor.

Her future lover.

Back in her room, she slipped into blue pajamas and lay in bed, but could not sleep. Instead, she tried to imagine the face of Jeremiah Taylor. Her eyes fluttered closed and she drifted off at last.

A deep male voice told her to enter his bedroom and undress. Then the disembodied voice ordered her to lie upon the bed.

"Open your legs," he said harshly.

Alexa kept them clamped shut.

"Open them wider. I wish to see you."

Burning with humiliation, she parted her legs. She tried to lift her head to see him, the one who would take her innocence, but his features were a blur.

Then she felt the mattress dip with his weight. The head of his penis bumped her inner thigh. It felt long and thick enough to accomplish the deed. Sweat beaded her temple and she clutched at the mattress.

Just do it, get it over with.

And then the head of his penis pushed at her entrance, nudged inside. It hurt. Alexa whimpered, but the bastard didn't care. He only wanted his conquest, the virgin he'd paid half a million for.

Do your duty ...

With a sneer, a contemptuous laugh and a grunt, he pushed deep inside, tearing her apart. The pain was

60

horrible and she screamed. He kept going, deep inside her, invading her body, so deep he would never get out, as the pressure between her legs became burning pain and she knew he wanted to grind himself so deep into her body, so no matter where she went or how many lovers she had he'd make certain she'd never, ever forget him...for he was stamped upon her soul...

Alexa woke up to sheets soaked with perspiration, a racing heart and the moonlight spilling upon the hardwood floor.

The mysterious billionaire had yet to show his face, or so she'd been told.

And yet the voice in her dream was familiar, icy cold and impervious.

Raphael's.

"When will you tell her the truth? I suspect she believes I am you," Raphael said.

Leaning against a tree trunk, Raphael watched J.J. throw a tennis ball against the house's wall and catch it. "She is not a stupid girl. Miss Grant deserves to know you are Jeremiah Taylor."

Usually bouncing a tennis ball against the wall soothed his over-active mind. Not tonight. J.J. felt restless and edgy, wanting the female who slept one floor below him.

"And you need to shut up. It's my business and I'll handle it."

"It becomes all our business, if you chose to mate with this young woman and she becomes our alpha female. This is not brokering a deal on your behalf, J.J.

61

Or attending a party, pretending to be you, the mysterious reclusive billionaire. This involves a young woman's heart."

And mine. "I know."

"This game you play will end in disaster if you do not take care."

"I want her to know the real me." He tossed the tennis ball against the wall. "She believes Jeremiah Taylor is a brutal, coldhearted ass."

"And I play the part brilliantly?"

J.J. studied Raphael's amused expression. "I need more time."

"You have six days, my friend. And then you must bed her. Will you tell her once you have her in your arms, sweetly seducing her? That is your plan, is it not? Seduce her with kisses and pleasure until it comes time to do the deed, and then she falls madly for you?"

J.J.'s chest tightened. Raphael knew him too well. But he did not know everything.

"If you do not tell her, perhaps I shall, before she grows so terrified of me the poor girl faints."

He crushed the tennis ball in his hand and turned to Rafe. "What?"

"Or perhaps I shall kiss her, and she will know when you take her that it is not me. Perhaps she shall prefer my kisses." Raphael gave a mocking smile. "Should I go to her bed to find out? I can play the part and do the deed for you."

The ruined tennis ball dropped to the ground as he reached out and slugged his beta in the mouth.

Raphael went down hard. He lay there, staring at the sky, unblinking.

"Come on you son of a bitch. Fight me. If you dare touch my Alexa…"

"I will not fight you, my friend. I made a promise to never hurt you," Raphael said quietly. "So you do have feelings and you are not toying with her."

Suddenly exhausted, he sat beside his beta. "Yeah. I do."

Raphael sat up and wiped his bloodied lip, examining the darkness on his fingers with a rueful look. "You still have a mean right hook. You could easily defeat your cousin if he challenged you for the right to keep Alexa in his pack."

Surprise filled him. "I told you that Daniel is my cousin?"

"You were drunk."

"Ah." J.J. picked up the destroyed tennis ball and bounced it in his palm. "I didn't tell you why I hate him so much?"

"No. That is your business."

He thought of Selena, her long chestnut hair just like Alexa's, the easy laugh that had turned mocking and cruel in the barn…

"I need you do something, Rafe. You're not going to like it."

"If it involves mucking out the stables, you are correct."

"Stay the fuck out of my business."

Raphael sighed. "As you wish. I agreed to obey you when I came into this pack. But take my advice, my friend. Alexa is smart. She will find out and the longer you avoid telling her, the worse it will be for both of you."

"I can't until I trust her."

63

"Then if you do not trust her, perhaps it is best not to tell her the truth." His friend's expression darkened, as if he remembered the bitter past. "You should get rid of her, before she ruins everything you cherish."

He threw the squashed tennis ball into the bushes. "I can't. I'm falling in love with her. How can I send her back when all I think about is Alexa?"

Raphael gave him a pitying look. "Love. The ruin of many a good Lupine. Love is not all sweetness and promise. It is dark and can destroy."

J.J. watched Raphael walk away, wondering if he was right.

CHAPTER 4

Four days to go.

She tried not to think of going to Jeremiah Taylor's bed and kept herself busy. J.J. helped. He asked her to haul water for the horses in the pasture, and help him fix fences. She'd fallen into the habit of joining him for breakfast and then, she went to the fitness room and walked on the treadmill until sweat popped on her forehead and her thighs burned.

Every night, she fell into bed exhausted. Yet her sleep remained restless.

Sometimes, she'd perch on the fence, gulping down water while watching him work with the horses. Every time J.J. bent over, the denim of his jeans hugging every inch of his tight butt, Alexa salivated.

Wow, he had a cute ass.

And he never stopped—she had to admire his work ethic. When she mentioned she needed things to do to work off her nervous tension, he asked for her help in organizing data on the ranch's new horse breeding program. J.J. brought a laptop into her room and mounds of papers he'd been "meaning to enter into the system."

"Help me find a better way of organizing this," he'd told her.

She'd lifted her brows and pointed at the papers. "Is that an order?"

J.J. had flashed that wicked cute grin. "It's my Jeremiah side coming out. I believe you can do it, and the skills you learned in college aren't being put to good use."

"Your Jeremiah side? What does that mean?"

He'd dropped the grin. "It's an expression around here. Means all business and ordering people around like an alpha."

"Have I told you I'm not very fond of alpha wolves?"

J.J.'s smile dropped and a hard look entered his eyes. "Jeremiah's a good alpha. He protects the pack, without stripping them of food like Daniel."

Late afternoon on the third day, Alexa felt exhausted. But she couldn't set aside the constant pace she'd worked over the past year. Too much guilt. Every single moment she rested felt like a waste of time.

So she set out for the organic garden near the main house. Gardening wasn't wasting time.

The square of earth boasted carrots, peas and cucumbers. Alexa knelt in the dirt, humming as she weeded. She pulled back her long hair and secured it with a clip.

Sunshine beat down upon her exposed nape. Sweat dripped down her back, pooled in the waistband of her jeans. At the garden's edge, a small gnome stood guard. In its faded red cap, green shirt, painted brown trousers and scuffed brown shoes with one toe missing, the gnome looked aged and worn. Its hands were clutched together as if holding a walking stick, but the stick was long gone. It guarded the garden with beady brown eyes, but had a sly look, a slit of a mouth sandwiched between a black beard and tiny mustache.

Someone else liked gnomes as she did.

J.J. galloped up on a chestnut gelding. Sitting back on her haunches, she admired the view. He slid off, let the reins trail and the horse began to crop grass near the tall oak tree.

He squatted by the gnome and tipped his hat back. She felt a tug of pure lust as she gazed at his lean face, that mouth that had delivered such pleasure in a few kisses.

She dusted off her hands. "That gnome is a little worn. Ever think of replacing it, or is Jeremiah too cheap to buy something as plebian as a garden statue?"

He patted the statue. "I salvaged this from my mama's garden. It's supposed to bring good luck. He's very special to me."

"Was that your Christmas bonus from Jeremiah? He let you put it in the garden?"

He gave her that odd look of his. It was as if she'd jerked back a curtain and saw another part of the wolf.

"Jeremiah is quite generous to friends. His enemies, not so much. He lets them know he doesn't dick around, especially if they abuse females under his protection."

"What does he do, eat them for breakfast?"

"He makes them regret their actions," he said darkly. "Speaking of food, Jane's making us a picnic dinner. Thought we'd eat at the guest house."

"Raphael isn't joining us?"

"He's in Durango for the night on a business

errand." J.J. squinted at the bright sun as she ran a shirtsleeve across her sweating forehead. "It's hot out here. You should rest."

"I'm fine." Alexa returned to digging in the earth. "I'm always fine. After I'm finished here, I'll work on those spreadsheets."

"You're overdoing it," he said gently. "And you're flushed. Go inside and cool down."

She couldn't stop. If she stopped, she'd start thinking about Sunday night and the apprehension would begin all over again. Ignoring him, she continued digging. Out of the corner of her eye she saw him stride over to her. Breath hissed out of her as J.J. scooped her into his arms.

"Put me down!"

"I told you, you're flushed and need to rest." He carried her to the guest house porch, and then into her room, settling her on the chair. J.J. headed into the bathroom and she heard the sound of water running in the bathtub.

Much as she hated to admit it, she *was* tired and hot. But back at Daniel's pack, if you didn't work, he found a reason to torment you.

"You're overbearing," Alexa snapped. "Has anyone ever told you that?"

"A few people," he called out. "It's my Jeremiah side coming out."

"And here I thought you were a nice guy."

J.J. emerged from the bathroom. "I am a nice guy. When people listen to me and obey."

"Obey?" She sputtered as he lifted her into his arms again. "I can walk."

"This feels better, having you in my arms."

He carried her into the bathroom, where water ran in the opulent tub. Bubbles foamed and popped and the fragrance of roses filled the air.

A bubble bath. Alexa wasn't accustomed to such luxury, only hasty showers in the morning, for she had to help her mother feed and dress her younger siblings.

J.J. set her on her feet and twisted the tap, turning off the water. He gave her a pointed look. "You're not here to work. You have three hours until dinner. Bath first and then a long nap. Now are you going to get undressed…"

J.J. pushed back his hat, his blue gaze gleaming, "or am I going to have to strip you naked?"

Alexa pointed to the door. "Out."

As he left, she slammed the door shut behind him and shouted, "I don't like your Jeremiah side."

A deep chuckle followed him out the room.

Alexa had to admit he was right. She'd been overheated and tired. The bubble bath had removed the tension from her body. And then she'd thought of J.J.'s strong body, his lean, handsome face and ran her hands over her body, wishing, wanting, longing…

Three hours later, she and J.J. sat on the back porch. Alexa dug into Jane's excellent beer-battered, fried-chicken strips and salad tossed in raspberry vinaigrette. Shadows shrouded the jagged mountains as the moon climbed into the velvet sky. A cool breeze flowed over them from the water, carrying the scent of freshly mown grass, hay, horses and J.J.'s delicious musk.

He smelled like a good time. He smelled like a wolf

69

on the prowl, but he treated her with respect. Still, she sensed an underlying current of danger about him, a quiet lethalness. Alexa wondered if under the armor she'd find the real J.J.

And what was it with the Jeremiah references?

Suspicion filled her. Alexa let her fork clatter to the empty plate. "You mend fences, farm, know how to use a backhoe and you're an expert rider. And for an ordinary cowboy, you have more than a touch of overbearing alpha. Anything else you're holding out on me? Like perhaps you *are* the alpha of this pack?"

J.J. lifted his shoulders. "I run this place like an alpha because I have the authority. Jeremiah is obsessed with business and making money. I have other skills, too. I'm an excellent lover. Want to find out?" He speared another cut of chicken and ate it, watching her face, which had to be red.

She wondered if it could possibly get any hotter.

"It's not polite to brag."

"Not bragging if it's the truth." J.J. pushed back his plate. Light from the flickering candles on the table played with the angles of his lean, handsome face.

His gaze locked with hers, as if he silently issued a challenge. A thrill raced through her. Was she up for this particular challenge? It wasn't learning to ride a horse, or operating a tractor, but the very sexual one a man issued to a woman he wanted in his bed.

And oh, she wanted to be there. Wanted her first time to be filled with tenderness, pleasure and desire, not the grinding, obligatory sex she'd be forced into Sunday night.

"You're probably a better lover than Jeremiah Taylor," she finally acknowledged.

J.J. chuckled, and the gleam in his eyes intensified. "You certain about that, *cariño*? Shall we find out?"

Alexa sucked down a quivering breath, but opted to keep it light. Because if this conversation kept going, she'd end up naked in J.J.'s bed. "Not tonight, dear. My thighs have a headache after all that bend and stretch in the garden. Losing my virginity isn't on the agenda. I'm already sore enough."

"Like I told you, the first time usually hurts for a woman, but the right lover can give you enough pleasure to forget the pain."

So much for keeping it light. His deep voice, cutting through the gurgle of the rushing river and the chorus of cicadas in the nearby trees, rubbed against her skin like velvet. A different ache arose in her, the ache to join her body to his.

"Getting chilly out. Let's build a fire in your bedroom," he suggested.

What kind of fire? This could be dangerous.

"The dishes..."

He waved a hand. "Jane already promised to clean up."

She'd experienced few pleasures over the past year since graduating from college, so she led the way through the French doors into her room.

J.J. saw the gnome on her bureau and picked it up. "Interesting. Did you buy this yourself?"

"It was a gift from my best friend, Jessica. She gave it to me as a good luck charm during our last semester finals."

"Only the statues, not real gnomes, bring good luck. My dad used to tell us stories about gnomes and how wicked they are, and difficult to catch. There's a myth that if a Lupine captures a gnome and puts it in a cage, the gnome can grant wishes just like a leprechaun."

Alexa frowned at the little statue. "I brought it here for luck, but it gives me the creeps lately. Like it's staring at me all the time and its eyes follow me around the room."

J.J. stared at the statue, seemingly lost in thought. "My cousin and I used to comb through the dark forest, searching to capture one. We were young and stupid."

"What did you wish for?" she asked.

"My cousin always wanted to be taller and more handsome. I always w-wanted..." he took a deep breath and said in rapid Spanish, "to be respected and have money."

As he replaced the statue, Alexa frowned. "I thought I placed him on the mantel. Maybe Jane moved him when she cleaned my room."

The best place for the gnome was the closet. After she put the gnome away, J.J. studied her.

"You must miss your family."

"I do, but it would be worse if I wasn't doing something to help them out."

A moment of weakness hit her like a sledgehammer. Alexa sank to the bed and stared at the fireplace as J.J. stacked wood in the hearth. "I don't want Sunday to arrive, but complaining about it won't change anything. But I wish I had more... you know."

He glanced over his shoulder. "Experience?"

She nodded.

"I can help you with that."

He joined her on the bed and slid a hand over the nape of her neck, his touch light. J.J. lowered his mouth to hers.

His kiss deeply aroused her. Alexa struggled against falling back into bed with him and saying the hell with Jeremiah Taylor.

She pushed away and stood on shaky legs, not trusting herself to surrender to her sensual instincts. "This isn't a good idea. I need to run tonight as wolf. Shake loose and be free."

"I'll join you."

Alexa shrugged, knowing he could hear her accelerated heartbeat. "I'm warning you, I'm a fast runner. I won't slow down to accommodate you," she told him as they went outside and headed down the steps.

J.J. grinned, his teeth showing very white and wolfish. "Wouldn't expect anything less."

A waxing moon shed silvery light upon the open fields and the river, and the thicket of trees across the water. Her wolf whined to bolt through the trees, then lope across the valley into the mountains. "Where are we headed?"

He studied her with his intense gaze. "Have you ever run in the mountains?"

No one had ever asked her before. When she ran as a wolf, the pack ran with her in small, designated spots. Daniel always dictated her moves, even in Lupine form. Another thrill of pleasure raced down her spine.

"Daniel forced us to run together. I refused to do anything with the pack. When I tried running alone, he punished me by locking me in my room. He kept trying to dictate my life."

J.J. leaned against a tree trunk. "You've never run just for the thrill of it with a partner who watches your back?"

She shook her head.

He held out his hand. "Come with me. I'll show you what it's like to be in a real wolf pack. You're avoiding your own nature."

She bristled at the criticism. "Trying to live apart has kept me from becoming as meek and mild as other followers."

"And you don't know if you're even cut out for leadership because you've been hiding from real pack life for too long."

He sounded cool and confident, and the statement poked a sore spot. "Better to avoid pack life than to follow an alpha around like a puppy dog."

"A good alpha can teach you much."

"There is no such thing as a good alpha. You seriously think Jeremiah Taylor is a good leader? Why? He's never even around."

J.J. stiffened. "He's a good leader who puts his people first."

"He's an alpha who thinks he can buy anything. Including me."

Breath whistled through his clenched teeth. "S-s."

Alexa frowned as he paused, ran a hand over his jaw. J.J. switched to Spanish. "Stop judging him so harshly."

"Why? Because he deserves it," she burst out in the same language. "Who buys a female for sex except someone who is so arrogant and uncaring as to think money can get him anything?"

"Maybe he heard of your situation with Daniel and wanted to offer an escape from that hellhole."

"Then offer me a job, give me money to pay off my student loan, but to buy me for the night?" The same helpless rage washed over her. "I'm not furniture. I'm my own person."

"You're the one who put yourself up for sale, honey."

"I had nothing else to sell!"

"There's no demand without supply. So give Taylor a chance."

Alexa had enough. She balled her hands into tight fists. "How many times has someone said that to me? Give this one a chance or give that one. First my parents—move here, Alexa, we can make a go of this. Let's go to this pack, Alexa. And then Daniel, bossing me around. I went to college to make something of myself and yet I'm stuck in the same position—letting others dictate my life." She drew in a quivering breath. "After Sunday night, I'm free to live my own life."

"Freedom isn't everything. The price you pay for it sometimes is loneliness." J.J.'s expression shuttered.

"Being alone is a good thing. Right now it's what I need. I've changed my mind. I'm running by myself."

"Not on my ranch. You don't know the turf. All kinds of traps lie out there for lone wolves." J.J. leaned close, got in her face so that she could count the bristles on his lean cheeks. His intensity scared her a little. Never had she met anyone so fiery, so filled with life and passion, and all of it directed at her.

"You've been riding solo for too long, Alexa. It's time someone took you in hand, showed you what it's like to be a real Lupine, living in a good pack."

"And you think you're that someone?" She backed up, refusing to lower her gaze. She'd never show submission. Daniel had hit her for her stubbornness, but time after time she'd risen, putting one foot in front of the other.

Because once they beat you down and you stayed down, you might as well give up.

She never gave up.

"I am. And you're going to learn. Starting tonight. You're running with me. I'll show you the best places for hunting game and wide, open spaces you'll love."

But she'd had enough of people forcing her hand. Her parents. Daniel. Soon, Jeremiah. Alexa kicked off the soft velvet slippers she'd worn to dinner, the shoes that disguised her blisters gotten in the fancy turquoise boots she'd worn to annoy him.

Her body was used to hurting.

Never again would she allow her pride to hurt, too.

"Try to stop me," she taunted and took off.

Alexa ran toward the bridge crossing the river. She called upon her magick and shifted as she raced over the wooden planks, feet becoming paws, her angry, sharp breath turning into howls. Thick fur covered her body. She smelled the night air, so cold and crisp, heard the scuttle of creatures in the undergrowth. Sensation overwhelmed her, like a rush of a drug. Her heightened senses enabled her to cut through the darkness and hear a pebble tumbling into the rushing river, smell old blood from an ancient kill.

Wildness filled her, along with the overwhelming urge to race through the fields and into the mountains, and never return.

She tore through the soft grass, into the woods, running, running, not caring where she went.

Wolf senses warned her that a predator was coming up fast from behind. J.J.? Swift and silent, she didn't catch his scent, but knew he followed, intending to catch her. Maybe bring her down as Daniel always did, mocking and humiliating her before everyone else. No one ever appreciated her, validated her existence.

She raced through field and brush, trampling clover, brambles tearing at her thick fur. Her paws scrabbled for purchase as she leapt onto a boulder and then clambered over it.

He caught her as she bolted forward, her lungs gasping for air, her tail held down to streamline the wind. She heard a tremendous whoosh and then he leapt upon her.

Alexa tumbled down to the earth, tasting dirt, tasting fear, hearing the roar of blood in her veins, seeing the moon sneer at her.

Always sneering at her, the lone wolf who dared to stand up to the alpha.

Howling, she dug her paws into the earth and snarled, struggling to escape the authority, the one who thought himself better, and wanted nothing more than to keep her down. Then the heavy weight upon her shifted a little. She felt his tongue lick her ear.

Suddenly the muscled wolf pinning her to the dank earth turned into a man's hard body. Confused, Alexa stopped struggling. A calloused hand pushed through her thick fur and a low voice murmured soothingly into her ear.

"Calm down, Alexa. It's okay. I won't hurt you. I'd never hurt you. I-I'd k-k."

A deep breath, then a volley of rapid Spanish. "I'd kill myself before hurting you and treating you like Daniel does. I want to help you, keep you safe. Understand? It's dangerous out here if you don't know the turf. There are coyotes, and stray hunters violating the No Trespassing signs. Snarl at me if you understand."

She managed a small snarl, still too stunned to do anything more. No male had ever cared about her welfare. In college, the few men she'd dated cared more about themselves, not her needs. They would leave her to walk alone back to her room. It had always amused her because if she ever felt truly threatened, she had her Lupine strength and powers to get her out of a jam. But it had bothered her just as much.

He chuckled. "That's my girl. My Alexa."

The hand pushing through her fur slowed, the strokes even and languorous. Her wolf whined, but not from fear or anger.

The man straddling her was naked.

A sudden desire pumped through her veins. Instinct took over. Alexa shifted back and rolled over. She remained naked, too. J.J. straddled her belly, his hands pinning her shoulders.

He stared down at her. Moonlight caressed the edges of his bristled jawline, shone in his blue eyes.

Rolling off her, he stood, tall, proud and quiet. Alexa scrambled to her feet.

She had never seen a naked man before. Even while running with the pack, rules were you shifted and then used your magick to immediately clothe yourself. No man was permitted to show his package to a female. Daniel controlled everything, even their nudity.

Stricken with shyness, she covered her breasts, unable to tear her gaze away from the muscles rippling along his torso, the faint line of dark hair marching down his belly to the thicker thatch at his groin, and his penis, now erect. A cloud drifted overhead, and the moon came out, showing J.J. in his full glory.

Huge. Once she'd caught a glimpse of Daniel's penis.

"Gerkin," she whispered.

J.J. raised his dark brows. "Did you just compare me to a tiny pickle?"

"Not you." Heat suffused her body and she was glad for the cover of night. "Daniel. He was … er, small."

"You saw him naked?" J.J. glowered. "Did he try to force himself on you?"

Smelling the anger radiating from his pores, she hastily reassured him. "No. I told you he wasn't interested in sex. He seemed to have trouble controlling his wolf magick when he shifted back."

J.J. frowned. "He's an alpha."

"He never fully had the powers of one. I never saw him with another woman, either. He didn't care about finding a mate. It was the only good thing about living in his pack. I never had to worry about his sexual advances. I don't know what I'd do if he touched me." She shuddered.

He gave her an intent look. "Are you scared of me, Alexa?"

Not of you. Of what my wolf wants to do with you. And that could be a very bad thing for my family.

"No." But she kept shielding her breasts with her hands.

He approached, his gaze filled with desire and tenderness. Never had a man looked at her this way. A few had mocked her weight in college. A few had dated her, saying, "You've got big, beautiful tits."

But none had ever looked at her this way, as if she

were the moon and the stars shining in his sole universe.

J.J. cradled her face in his hands. "You are so lovely in the moonlight, like a dream come to life."

His kiss was soft and sweet. As she dropped her hands and leaned into him, he deepened the kiss. Then he pulled away, searching her face.

"Don't hurt me. I've been hurt enough," she whispered.

A smile touched his sensual mouth. "I would never hurt you, *cariño*. You are far too precious to me."

Cupping the nape of her neck with one strong hand, he kissed her again. J.J. sampled her mouth, running his tongue along the generous curve of her lips. Alexa clung to his shoulders as his tongue leisurely thrust past her lips. Her mouth opened under the subtle, demanding pressure of his. Desire suffused her and she drew closer, wanting more.

When he broke the kiss she stared at him in the moonlight. His body was splendid. Thick, wavy hair black as midnight spilled over his forehead. Alexa imagined tunneling her fingers through the locks as he pleasured her with his mouth.

Firm muscles outlined his arms and legs. A wealth of crisp, dark hair covered his rippled chest, arrowing down his hard stomach to the thick nest at his groin. Alexa stared in fascination and unease at the large, stiffened penis jutting out, its rounded head pointing upward.

He was huge. She could not imagine taking that steely length inside her.

J.J. sank to the ground, and held out a hand.

Alexa hugged herself, torn between sensual need and

common sense. "If I'm not a virgin when I go to Jeremiah's bed, the contract is broken."

Hunger and tenderness shone in his gaze as he looked at her. "I promise you, you will be a virgin when you go to him."

Her wolf howled to join him. Alexa went to the ground and he took her into his arms, his heat a blanket of warmth in the cold night. They kissed again, their tongues tangling in heated pleasure and she lost all coherent thought. J.J. slid a palm down to her hip, sending sizzling currents through her body with each gentle stroke. He dropped tiny, quick kisses over her chin, neck, and collarbone, then down to her tender breasts. He cupped their heavy weight in his palms, encircling her aching nipples with his thumbs.

Desire darkened his gaze as it swept over her. Alexa dragged in a deep breath, stunned at the feelings overwhelming her. So this was passion, the sweet tension between her thighs intensifying with each flick of his thumbs. Moisture flooded her passage as his lips replaced his hand. J.J. licked her cresting nipple very slowly. Then he took it fully into his mouth and suckled deeply. His tongue flicked rapidly as she pumped her hips upward. She wanted him inside her, plunging hard and deep, sealing her to him.

But she must save herself for another.

J.J. caressed her belly, tunneled into the thick, dark curls covering her mound. Alexa moaned as he slid a finger across her slick, wet cleft. She stiffened as he thrust a finger inside her narrow sheath. He inhaled sharply as his finger butted against her hymen. Then he gently began small, intimate thrusts as his thumb circled her clit. She twisted and moaned as at each stroke, sweet tension building to painfully sharp pleasure. Alexa felt consumed, aching as the fires built to an incredible tension.

She writhed beneath him, moaning. This was the sensual nature of the Lupine, the call of flesh to flesh. Not the impersonal, cold demand of a billionaire who wanted her body for one night, who purchased her innocence as he purchased stocks and bonds. This was wild and freeing and natural.

Her wolf rose up, clawing eagerly in need.

Then J.J. pushed his hands between her thighs and lowered his head. Alexa sat up and squeaked.

"What are you doing?"

J.J. lifted his head. "You smell like coconuts. I want the taste of you beneath my tongue. Let me taste you, Alexa."

"I can't do this!"

Immediately, he stopped and sat back on his haunches. "What's wrong?"

"This. You. Everything." She gulped down a breath. "It's too much."

"Have you ever orgasmed before?"

The question made her face heat, the cool wind failing to fan the blush from her cheeks. "What kind of question is that?"

"We're a sensual people, we Lupines. Simply because you're a virgin doesn't mean you haven't experienced one. Have you ever pleasured yourself?"

Now the flush turned volcanic. "I, ah..."

"Truth, Alexa."

"Um..."

"Tell me," he coaxed her gently. "There's nothing to be ashamed of, not with me."

"Ah...this afternoon." Wind rustled the overhead leaves as it sighed through the trees. "In the bathtub... I thought of you."

She'd pleasured herself, imagining J.J.'s face, intent with passion, as he stared down at her, his body sinking heavily into hers.

"Did you have an orgasm?"

At the hasty jerk of her head, male satisfaction glinted in his eyes. "Then allow me to give you another." His gaze gleamed in the moonlight. "Let me pleasure you, Alexa."

And if you do, then I'll want you even more and I can't risk my heart getting broken, wanting to stay here with you. I have to focus on my goals and my family.

"I can't," she whispered.

Scrambling to her feet, Alexa fled back toward the bridge. But she had run south, and would have to walk back to the main bridge. She spotted a small footbridge and ran toward it.

It looked old, but safe. Alexa stepped onto it.

Halfway across, one of the planks sagged. Panicking, she tried to sprint forward, but the boards beneath her collapsed.

Alexa fell straight into the churning, icy water.

CHAPTER 5

Screaming, Alexa flailed her arms, struggling to stay afloat in the dark, wicked current. Needles of cold stabbed her naked skin.

She heard J.J. shout, and then another loud splash. Suddenly two strong arms wrapped around her. "Alexa, stop fighting, let me tow you," he shouted.

Instinct warred against it, but she fought the urge to keep thrashing and allowed him to tow her to the sandy shoreline.

J.J. carried her out of the water and she sat on the river bank, shuddering from the cold. He wrapped his arms around her, giving her his body heat.

Together they climbed the embankment. J.J. rubbed her arms briskly. "I had that footbridge fixed last week. Someone must have screwed around with the repairs. There will be hell to pay."

When they reached her room, J.J. herded her into the shower. Still shivering, she glanced behind her as he stepped into the enclosure and shut the glass door.

J.J. turned on the hot water and let it sluice over her skin, then ran a soapy washcloth over her back. There was nothing sexual in the way he washed her. It was businesslike, but gentle.

When she'd stopped shivering at last, and the hot water turned lukewarm, he shut it off and toweled her off gently as she stepped out. Then he snagged a big white terrycloth bathrobe from the door hook and helped her into it. J.J. rubbed himself dry and then clothed himself by magick.

"You okay?" he asked.

At her nod, he gave her a thoughtful look. "Dry your hair. I'll make hot chocolate."

Minutes later, they sat on chairs before the roaring fire in her room, mugs of hot chocolate cupped in their hands. J.J. had dressed in jeans and a baseball shirt, covering that amazing body. Her wolf howled in pure female frustration, but her Skin side knew it was for the best.

Alexa finished her chocolate, swallowing past the thick lump in her throat. "I wish I'd never gone to college and put myself in this financial bind. Or at least didn't save my virginity for a mate. How stupid is that? I save myself for love, and then sell myself to pay off a loan."

He took both empty cups, set them down, and knelt by her side. "Alexa, I promise you that Jeremiah Taylor is not a beast. He's not cruel or unkind."

"What are you trying to tell me, J.J.?"

"Tomorrow. I'll tell you tomorrow."

She wanted to trust him, believe him. "You say he's like that, but how can I know you're telling the truth?"

"He's a good man." J.J. enfolded her hands in his. "He'd never hurt you."

Too exhausted to argue, she shook her head. "I wish

I could believe you." Alexa leaned back and closed her eyes. "When I hit the water, I panicked. Silly me. I'm a good swimmer."

"You had good reason to panic. That current was ripping. Most people would have been afraid of drowning."

"I'm not afraid of drowning. I'm more afraid of spiders. I once walked into a nest of them back at Daniel's place. Ever since, I've been terrified of spiders. Stupid, huh? A wolf afraid of spiders."

J.J. touched her cheek. "Everyone's afraid of something. Get some sleep. I'll make sure no spiders invade your room."

She gave a sleepy smile and settled back against the chair, feeling her eyelids close. "You rock, J.J. Why couldn't you be Jeremiah Taylor? Then everything would be all right."

Alexa deserved the truth. And she'd have it, soon.

After 15 minutes passed, she finally fell asleep in the chair. J.J. lifted Alexa into his arms, and settled her into the bed. He sat on the edge, stroking her silky hair. So lovely and courageous. A perfect mate for an alpha.

An alpha who hid his real identity.

His conscience pricked. Could she truly be aligned with Daniel? He could trust her. Alexa detested her alpha.

But memories of Selena's taunts and rejection haunted him. He wanted to trust Alexa, but had to make certain of her intentions. The truth would come out soon enough.

J.J. dropped a kiss on her forehead, checked the room for stray cobwebs and the tiniest threat lurking in the corner. No spiders. He snapped out the lights and closed the door behind him. He headed upstairs to his temporary bedroom, sat by the fireplace and stretched out his long legs.

He had it all. And yet he had nothing, for he had no mate to share it with.

When he'd first struck out on his own, before he'd founded his pack, he'd lived alone in Colorado. He'd spent his days buying and trading stock, and nights running with the moon at the local park. But it was a lonely life without a pack.

"You don't want to know the life of a lone wolf, Alexa," he murmured. "I have."

He yearned for a mate who'd share more than her body. He wanted her to share her hopes and dreams and life, her laughter and her tears.

Alexa was that female. But what if she turned out to be like Selena, with her sly laugh and her cruel pleasure in humiliating him?

And how could he coax Alexa to open up and be honest when he wasn't being totally honest in return?

A scream sounded downstairs. J.J. bolted out of his room, taking the steps two at a time. He burst into Alexa's room and snapped on the overhead light.

She sat up in bed, scrubbing her smooth cheek, her face pale. "Someone touched my face. It felt horrid, like these small hands stroking over my skin. Like spider legs."

He searched the room, but found nothing. J.J. sat on the bed and smoothed back her hair. "It was a nightmare."

She shivered again. "But it felt so real!"

"I'll make sure your doors are locked." He dropped a kiss atop her head. "Try to get some rest. I'll be close by."

A nightmare. Of course. But before he closed the French doors and locked them tight, he saw something on the terrace, highlighted by the waxing moon.

J.J. went outside, squatted down and examined the marks.

Tiny, muddy footprints, as if a gnome had walked across the terrace....straight into Alexa's room.

Two hours later, after he'd inspected every corner, ensured nothing could hurt Alexa and she was deeply asleep, J.J. went to his room and finally collapsed into an exhausted slumber.

He dreamt of his past.

Eleven years old, fishing with Daniel. His cousin had invited him and, hoping to regain the old friendship, he'd gone with him to the lake. Sunshine beat down on the silvery water, heating his neck. J.J. used a lure, but Daniel hooked a slimy leech on his pole. J.J. tried not to look. He hated bloodsuckers.

"You're never going to feed your pack when you grow up if you use that." Daniel pointed to the lure and scoffed. "You need leeches."

He'd hesitated, and spoke in a small voice. "I, I d-don't have any."

"There's some in the cooler. Jeez, must I do everything?"

J.J. set down his pole and trudged to the blue cooler, big as a coffin. He opened the lid.

It was filled with stinky muck and hundreds of squirming, slimy leeches. Licking his lips, he reached inside to pluck one free.

Someone pushed him, hard and he fell inside the cooler. The lid slammed shut. J.J. screamed as the leeches slithered over his skin.

"Get out cuz! If you stay in there much longer, they'll suck away your balls. Leeches love Lupine balls!"

J.J. screamed and pounded at the cooler lid, but Daniel sat on it, laughing, laughing, laughing...

He awoke in a cold sweat, his heart racing. Gods, he hadn't had that nightmare in years. Stuck in that cooler for what seemed like hours, screaming until his throat grew hoarse and his uncle finally freed him. Big, bloodied welts on his bare legs, one near his upper thigh...

Wiping his forehead with the edge of the sheet, he felt movement in the bed.

Something wet and slimy on his thigh. Near his balls...

Horror pulsed through him. J.J. tore back the covers with a cry of disgust and jumped out of bed.

He always slept nude. Tonight was no exception.

Clinging to his muscled upper right thigh was a fat, slimy black leech. Fingers trembling, he plucked it off and threw it down.

His own blood splattered on the floorboards.

J.J. tore back the covers. Dirt and mud fouled the clean white sheets. Wriggling on the mattress were dozens of black, wet leeches with tiny gaping mouths.

Bile rose in his throat.

Daniel knew how much he hated leeches. Knew his

greatest fear was being buried alive with those slippery bastards curling next to his flesh, trying to burrow inside him…their little teeth sucking his blood…

He was not that terrified child anymore. Growling, J.J. raced to the dresser, grabbed the ice bucket and began scooping the leeches inside. When the last bloodsucker was flushed down the toilet, and the bed stripped and replaced with fresh sheets, he showered, dressed in sweat pants and then called Rafe and told him what happened.

J.J. opened the downstairs door and let in his beta.

Rafe studied the dirty sheets J.J. had dumped on the floor. Beneath his beard, his jaw tensed. "I checked the door locks. Everything was locked. The intruder had to have accessed the building while hiding in one of the rooms."

"Tomorrow I want new security cameras in front of my room and Alexa's. If someone enters or leaves, I want to know."

His beta's mouth compressed. "Have you considered that Alexa's hatred of Daniel is an act?"

J.J.'s worst fear soured in his belly. "That makes no sense."

Rafe thoughtfully regarded him. "None of us knew of your disgust for leeches. Who else knows?"

"Only Daniel," J.J. admitted.

"And perhaps Daniel shared that knowledge with someone in his pack. A certain female Lupine whose virginity you purchased."

"Why?"

"Revenge. Perhaps Daniel discovered you were the one who financially ruined him…and as a consequence, ruined Alexa and her family as well and made their lives miserable. He could be forcing her into spying for him, threatening her family if she does not comply."

J.J. hated the thought, which he'd harbored himself in his darkest dreams. But as Rafe had pointed out, the doors were locked from the inside.

He wanted to trust Alexa. But how could he? "You're very suspicious," he told Rafe.

The beta shrugged. "I swore an oath of loyalty to protect you while I remain in this pack. I must look after your best interests. And you know me, my friend. I do not trust easily."

Sighing, J.J. nodded. "Get some sleep. We have a lot of work tomorrow."

After the beta left, J.J. remained staring into the empty fireplace, wondering about Alexa.

Much as he wanted to dismiss the thought, it rested there like a nasty thing, wriggling inside his brain.

Like a fat, squirming leech.

No way could he risk telling Alexa the truth right now about his identity.

Because he didn't know if she was aligned with Daniel, and would turn on him in the end.

Just like Selena had...

Remembering how she'd tossed her hair, just like Selena, and glanced away, he felt his chest ache. How could he be certain Alexa wasn't loyal to Daniel? Pack was pack. He knew how loyal his Lupines were. What if Daniel commanded the same loyalty of Alexa, just as he'd held Selena's?

What if Daniel had found out J.J. was Jeremiah and sent Alexa here to sabotage the ranch?

He wasn't certain yet. But he knew one thing. He

must keep a closer eye on Alexa. J.J. frowned. Tomorrow he had to catch up on business. He'd send Raphael to watch over her.

As much as he longed to trust Alexa with the truth, he couldn't yet.

CHAPTER 6

She didn't see J.J. at breakfast the next day. He didn't show up for lunch, either. Jane apologized, saying J.J. had a lot of work to do.

The housekeeper hadn't met her gaze and muttered excuses about having work when Alexa tried pressing her for answers.

Clearly J.J. was avoiding her. But why? Because he didn't want to get sexually involved with her, knowing she was destined for Taylor's bed? Her instinct warned that wasn't the reason. J.J. was a strong male who exercised control.

No, something else was wrong.

And in the absence of J.J., there was Raphael, who kept dogging her like a wolf after prey. He didn't share meals, but appeared in the dining room, politely inquiring if she had any concerns.

Raphael's hovering added to her suspicions. The beta probably was Jeremiah Taylor. Because the mysterious Jeremiah Taylor had not shown up. Not even a stray scent or a hint of the billionaire.

After working on the spreadsheets for the ranch, Alexa decided to look for the missing J.J. They needed to talk. She wasn't a tease. And she needed to make it clear that she could be nothing more than friends with him until after Sunday night.

Alexa changed into clean jeans, a yellow short-sleeved shirt and sneakers, and went outside to search for J.J. Near one of the horse corrals, Raphael was lounging against the gate, staring into space. His Stetson was tipped back on his head and his jeans and blue work shirt looked dusty.

"Raphael, do you know where J.J. is?"

The beta turned. Unease arrowed through her. Raphael's eyes looked beadier and his mouth crooked downward in an ugly sneer. Remembering her theory that the beta was really Jeremiah Taylor, Alexa took a step back.

Maybe he'd heard of their interlude while running last night and didn't like it...

She tried for a friendly tone, although his expression didn't warrant one. "Whatcha doing?"

"Repairing the broken gatepost."

It didn't look broken, but she didn't want to spend any additional time getting explanations. "Where's J.J.?"

A nasty smile touched his mouth. "He's in the storage shed by the barn, cleaning it out for the new tractor. Need directions, sweetheart?"

She wouldn't ask directions from him if she was lost in the Sahara and he knew the nearest oasis. The beta looked dangerous and cruel, as if she'd interrupted him in a secret pastime of plucking wings off flies. The wind blew and she caught a very faint odor. The Lupine smelled like he'd been sweating and it was not pleasant.

Alexa muttered thanks and hurried away, feeling his gaze burn into the back of her shirt.

The fire-engine red barn stood out like an exclamation point among the green pastures, dwarfing the small weathered storage shed beside it. No bigger than a walk-in closet, the shed looked abandoned with disuse. Why would J.J. waste time cleaning it out when there was an entire barn to store farm equipment?

She opened the door.

Darkness met her. Alexa toggled the light switch on the wall. Nothing.

The shed smelled musty with disuse. "J.J.?"

She took a tentative step inside. Out of the corner of her eye, she saw a tall cowboy with a white Stetson and a mulberry shirt approach from the side. J.J.

But as she turned, he gave her a rough push. Alexa tumbled into the shed. The door slammed shut.

Alexa sprang to her feet and jiggled the rusty doorknob and found it locked. "J.J.! Let me out. Now!"

A high-pitched giggle came from outside. The sound sent a chill rushing down her spine. Where had she heard that nasty sound before?

She pressed all her weight against the door. It was bolted from the outside.

"J.J.!"

Disbelief filled her. Why was he doing this? Was he that upset with her? He'd been nothing but kind last night, staying with her until she fell asleep again after her nightmare.

Soft sounds scuffled in the darkness. Sweat trickled down her temples as her heart pounded faster.

She took a step back and felt the soft, silken caress of something sticky upon her cheek. And then

95

something crawled upon her head, hesitated, and then continued down to her forehead.

Spider...

Alexa beat at her head, screaming. Arms flailing, she tore at a net of webs. More spiders descended upon her fingers, delicate legs crawling up her bare arms. Oh gods, they were headed for her face, her face...

She screamed louder and her wolf instincts howled. Alexa shifted and barreled for the door.

Snarling, tail tucked down, her wolf crashed into the door. Wood splintered and cracked from the heavy impact. Alexa ran faster, into the sunshine, then dropped to a patch of grass, rubbing her muzzle against it, trying to free herself of cobwebs and crawling things...

The horse trough!

Panting, she raced forward and landed in the water with a loud splash. Alexa shifted back and scrubbed her naked body, her hair, gods, they were in her *hair*!

Finally she stepped out of the water, dripping on the dirt, and dressed herself by magick. Her clothing was soaked, her hair was sopping.

With a shaky hand she wrung out her long hair and rubbed a hand against her face, reassuring herself that no spiders crawled down her cheek.

J.J. rounded the barn corner, saw her and stopped short. "Alexa? What the hell's going on? Why are you wet? You okay?"

Okay? He looked confused as she sidestepped his hand.

"You should know! You locked me in there!"

"What?"

"The shed! You locked me inside the shed. There

were spiders everywhere." Alexa couldn't stop shaking. "I broke out and ran for the water to get them off me!".

He drew away, a frown denting his dark brows. "I was nowhere near the shed. Rafe and I were inspecting the riding trails. Someone has been digging potholes and trying to trip the horses. No one's been inside that shed for years. I've been meaning to tear it down."

"I saw you! Same white hat, jeans, mulberry shirt..."

J.J. plucked at the fabric of his long-sleeved shirt. "This is red."

"For Danu's sake, red, mulberry, doesn't matter! It was you! Why did you lock me inside? I told you I hated spiders!"

"Alexa, it was not me." He spoke very slowly, as if speaking to a small child.

Deeply shaken, she wanted to scream and beat at his chest with her fists. How could he manipulate her like this? The same male who'd rescued her from the river?

"I don't know what kind of sick game you're playing, but it ends now. I'm stuck here on this damned ranch for the next few days until I fulfill the terms of my contract. Get used to it and until I leave, stay out of my way."

Her bare feet made squishing noises on the grass as she stomped off, leaving J.J. to stare after her.

After a long, hot shower (first checking the shower stall for hidden spiders) Alexa changed into yoga pants and a white T-shirt and sneakers, took a towel and headed to the fitness center to walk and think. She was deeply stricken at the idea that J.J. had locked her into the shed, and then denied doing so.

She thought he was her friend. She'd wanted him to become her lover. But now she wasn't certain.

The center wasn't vacant. Raphael sat on a gray bench, working out with weights. Him again.

In a black T-shirt and gray sweats, he nodded. Alexa pulled her hair back into a ponytail and secured it with a clip.

"I thought you were fixing the broken gatepost by the small corral."

Raphael glanced up.

"After lunch, I was inspecting the horse trails, before coming here. There's no broken gatepost."

"But you told me it was broken and you had to fix it. Just like you told me J.J. was in the storage shed…"

Her voice trailed off.

"Something wrong, princess?"

It made no sense. Unless he had a twin.

"You must have a doppelganger. Someone is running around the ranch, imitating you."

She expected him to laugh or shake his head. Instead he set down the weights and pinned her with a severe look. "Tell me."

Alexa told him everything. Raphael quietly swore.

"Did my twin have a very faint, odd odor, like rotting fish?"

Her nose wrinkled. "Not rotting fish, but a little smelly, like body odor. I thought it was strange because Lupines don't smell like that. The Skins I dated in college smelled like that. It was pretty putrid."

As the beta sat on the bench, looking thoughtful, she selected the treadmill she'd been using all week and began walking. Sweat trickled down her backside. Raphael made her deeply nervous, but if he was Jeremiah Taylor, maybe he liked manipulating her. She needed to poke him, see what she could discover. Alexa gathered her courage.

"It's a nice gym you have here. Very generous of Mr. Taylor to build it for the hired help. Maybe he's not as much of a skinflint as I've heard."

Yep, start the conversation out with a jab. See what she hit.

The beta tilted his head. "Why do you hate him for being rich?"

"Oh, I don't hate him, just despise him for throwing his money around and buying me for one night as if I'm merchandise." Alexa put the treadmill on a faster speed, at a higher incline.

"Do you hate all Mexicans? Do you hate me for being Mexican?"

She glanced at him, puzzled. "Of course not."

"I'm not Mexican. I'm from Italy."

"But you said you were from Mexico..." Alexa flushed.

"I said I lived in Mexico. That doesn't make me Mexican any more than being rich makes Jeremiah heartless. He's the most generous, compassionate Lupine I know. And you are the one who put yourself up for auction, princess."

Alexa fell silent. Had she prejudged Jeremiah because of gossip and conjecture? She'd always considered herself fair. But there was the matter of the auction...

"If he's so compassionate and generous, why did he purchase me for one night in his bed?"

Raphael approached, a hank of sweat-dampened black hair hanging in his eyes. He pushed it back with an impatient hand as he stood next to the treadmill. "Perhaps he heard of your troubles and wanted to help. And this was the only way."

"He could have paid off my debt."

"Your alpha wouldn't allow it. And perhaps Jeremiah finds you attractive and desirable. He is a male, after all."

Now the flush spread like wildfire through her body. She wasn't getting anywhere with this machine. The treadmill or the Lupine she'd confronted.

"You're his beta. So you'd defend him, no matter what."

"I'd give my life for him," Raphael said quietly. He looked intense, dangerous.

Curiosity filled her. "What did he do to inspire such loyalty?"

Raphael rolled his shoulders. "I ran into a little trouble. If not for J...Jeremiah, I'd be bleached bones by now."

"Trouble over what?"

Silence fell between them. She caught a scent of male sweat and spice, and something deeper. Not fear, but deep-seated pain.

"It's not my business," she said gently, sensing he did not want to talk about it.

Those broad shoulders lifted. "It matters not. You will discover it sooner or later."

Sooner or later? What did that mean?

As Raphael removed his shirt, she tensed with apprehension. Of course she'd find out. If he was Jeremiah Taylor, he'd be naked with her on Sunday evening. A triangle of black hair covered his chest and muscles lined his flat torso. He was quite handsome. Then he turned around to show her his back.

"They put salt in the wounds to ensure I'd scar," he said flatly.

Her stomach gave a sickening twist. "Dear goddess, who could be that cruel?"

"There are many out there, princess." Raphael put his shirt back on and glanced at her, his gaze hard as steel. "I don't take lightly to anyone disparaging the alpha of this pack, not even his woman."

"I'm not his woman!"

Raphael's gaze swept over her body in a lingering caress. "You will be soon."

Alexa's hands shook. Now more than ever, she was convinced Raphael was Jeremiah Taylor. Gods, she wanted to race out of here and run as far away as possible.

Her guts twisted into knots as she thought about lying with Raphael and giving him her virginity. He seemed dangerous and hinted of dark secrets and mystery. Cold sweat dripped down her back. How could she give herself to this aloof Lupine? She'd wanted her first time to be filled with passion, not fear.

Raphael was totally opposite of J.J., who made her heart beat faster, her body grow warm and pliant.

Alexa made a note to call Jessica. Her friend knew how to hack any computer system. If anyone could confirm Raphael was Taylor, it was Jessica.

The gym door opened and J.J. entered, a white towel slung around his broad shoulders. He headed for a treadmill near her, stepped on it and removed his towel, draping it over one railing. Alexa's apprehension turned to grief. She'd trusted him last night, and he'd pulled that stunt with the shed. And thought she was crazy in her accusations.

Raphael glanced at her. "J.J. Your friend Alexa here said I have a twin running about the ranch. Apparently my twin told her to enter the shed where she had the nasty encounter with the spiders."

J.J. frowned. "The same shed you said I locked you into?"

Alexa nodded.

The Lupine glanced at her. "So maybe I have a twin, too? Because I sure didn't lock you into a shed. Rafe, check it out. I want to know what the hell's going on around here. First the leeches last night..."

"Leeches?" Her stomach turned.

"Nothing for you to worry about."

"I will find the culprit. If there is an intruder, he will regret it," Raphael said darkly.

Alexa watched him pick up his towel and head for the weights on the opposite side of the gym. With his arrogant swagger and confidence, she knew he was an alpha.

J.J. started the machine and began jogging.

Raphael was handsome, she admitted. He had a physique of solid muscle, strong and sure. But J.J. was lean with the coiled strength of steel cord. Blue gaze intent, he stared straight ahead as he ran. Clad in a tight gray T-shirt and black shorts, he made the run look easy. Dark hair covered his muscled forearms and long limbs.

Warmth spread through her as she watched him, thinking about all that male strength, his solid muscled body as he lay atop her, his ass pumping firmly not from running, but from thrusting deep inside her.

Stop thinking about sex. You don't know this guy, can't trust him. First he wants to make love to you by the river, then he avoids you and then locks you into a shed. Stay away. He's bad news.

But not until she found out what he'd wanted to tell her.

"You said you needed to tell me something today," she told him.

"Changed my mind."

"Why?"

"Eventually it will leech out."

Frustration filled her. She needed answers, not jokes. "Talk to me, J.J. Does this have to do with our shifting last night? With what happened in the woods? Is that why you locked me in the shed, because you were mad at me for some silly reason?"

"Alexa, I did not lock you in the shed. But it's obvious someone did and I will find out what the hell is going on. We'll talk later. It's been a long day and I need to run."

"Fine. You're just as arrogant and unfeeling as Raphael."

J.J. shook his head. "Rafe is a good Lupine. He has reasons for being as he is."

Had reasons for playing games and hiding his real identity? Just as J.J. had reasons for locking her in the shed with the spiders?

Get me out of here. I need air.

Alexa pressed the stop button.

Nothing happened.

She pressed it again. Nothing. She reached for the

remote control, dangling from the treadmill from a slim red cord.

And then the cord holding the remote snaked through the air, slid around her neck, tickling her skin.

Alexa pulled it away. What kind of sick magick was this?

The red cord pulled tight around her neck.

Gasping, she struggled to free herself, feeling her air supply cut off.

The machine picked up speed, but she was trapped by the cord. Alexa gasped for oxygen, her legs forced to pump faster as her already straining lungs tried to pull in air. "Help," she choked out.

Tears flooded her eyes as she tried to pull free, her vision graying. A loud snarl filled the air and out of the corner of her eye, she saw J.J.'s claws emerge.

Oh gods, he was going to finish her off. The shed was a preview. Now he planned to really hurt her. Maybe kill her. Alexa thrashed harder, desperate to free herself. Panic iced her veins as she fought with the chord, edged away from those sharp claws that could slice her to ribbons.

"Stop struggling! Stay still or I'll cut you!"

With his claws, J.J. slashed downward, slicing through the cord imprisoning her and then he smashed the treadmill's casing.

Before the machine ground to a halt, he lifted her into his arms, ripping the cord from her neck. He cradled her against his chest so close she heard his thumping heartbeat. Raphael ran over to them.

"Rafe, what the hell's going on here?" J.J. snapped.

Raphael ripped open the machine and examined the

motor. "Someone warded this treadmill with dark magick."

"A blind troll could have told me that. Who? Damnit, I want to know who!"

"Patience, patience," Raphael murmured.

"I have none. Find out."

Raphael looked up. "What, you will fire me?"

He can't fire you, because you're the alpha. Gods, she needed fresh air. Her head ached and her throat hurt.

Ignoring him, J.J. left the fitness room, Alexa in his arms. He gently set her down outside and then examined her throat.

A low growl rumbled deep in his chest as he gently probed the line stretching across her neck. "I could kill whoever is responsible for hurting you."

"I'll be fine," she rasped, fighting the urge to cry from the pain and shock. Everything was collapsing, and she felt crazy, her emotions in a lather. But no one ever saw her cry.

"I would never hurt you. Ever. I have no reason to lock you in a shed with spiders and I sure as hell didn't make the cord wrap around your throat." J.J.'s lean cheeks flushed with angry color. He cupped her cheeks. "But I swear, I'll find whoever did this and make him pay for hurting you. Someone is fucking with you, and I'll have his balls in a vise."

Pulling her into his arms, he rubbed her back in long, soothing motions. Lupines needed touch, craved it. And his touch was beginning to calm her, quell the hysteria that had taken over.

After a few minutes, he eased away and gazed down at her, his blue eyes filled with concern. "Better now?"

Alexa nodded.

J.J. touched her cheek, rubbing his thumb across her clammy skin. "Do you believe that I'd never pull stunts like that?"

Her throat felt as if she'd swallowed sandpaper. "I want to," she whispered.

J.J.'s mouth thinned. "Let's get you back."

He walked with her to the guest house. Inside, he made her sit in the living room while he fetched her a glass of ice water. The liquid felt cool against her sore throat.

Pacing the room, he laced his hands behind his back. "Those treadmills are inspected every week. Whoever warded the one you used must have done it this morning."

Alexa set down the glass with a shaky hand. "Up until the time you freed me, I thought it might have been you."

The stunned surprise in his eyes almost made him look comical. "Me? Why?"

"Because you've done everything to avoid me today and then there was the shed incident." Alexa coughed and rubbed her throat. "I thought you were angry at me for rejecting you. Oh gods, my head hurts thinking about it. No, my throat hurts more."

"Hush." He knelt before her and pressed a gentle finger against her lips. "Don't talk anymore."

Then he sat back and sighed, running a hand through his hair. "Someone is trying to split us apart."

"Who?"

"Someone who thinks you and I are together too much and wants us each to place blame on the other." Taking her hand, he stared at her, his expression stricken. "I would never hurt you, *cariño*. I'd strangle

106

myself before I did that. I care about you and it makes me furious to think someone wants you to think I'm the guilty one."

Sincerity filled his deep voice and as she searched his face, Alexa realized he told the truth. J.J. couldn't have done this.

As his arms came around her waist, she hugged him back, feeling broken and lost.

"Whoever did this is making me hurt more than just physically. Because it already hurts so much, knowing I can't have you. I can't get close to you because I can't even think past what will happen Sunday night," she whispered.

He closed his eyes, brought her hands to his mouth and kissed her knuckles. "No one's going to hurt you anymore, Alexa. I promise this, I will do whatever I must to keep you safe."

"Even from Jeremiah Taylor? What if he's the one playing these pranks?"

J.J. dragged in a deep breath. He seemed to be struggling with a decision. Finally he looked at her. "He isn't. Trust me, he is not like that. You'll know soon. But right now, I'm worried you're overwrought and upset. You need rest."

He stood and pulled her to her feet. When they reached her room, he escorted her inside, checked the doors and the closet and then ran a hand through his hair, his expression grim.

"I'm sleeping here tonight. My wolf will protect you. No one's going to lay a hand on you. If they dare try, I'll tear them to shreds."

J.J. shifted into a wolf and lay on the floor by the French doors.

Later, Jane brought them both dinner, a chicken pot pie for her, and raw steak for him. Still in wolf form, he gobbled it down.

When she woke in the middle of the night, he was gone. And then she peered out the windows and saw him resting outside as a wolf, his head on his paws, keeping watch.

The thought comforted her as she drifted back to sleep, even as suspicion nagged her.

Why would someone wish to break them apart, if it wasn't the mysterious Jeremiah Taylor? Who else would even care?

CHAPTER 7

She felt much better by Thursday morning, but J.J. ordered her to stay in the guest house and relax. Alexa spent the hours organizing financial information for the ranch, and texting with Molly and Jessica. Gentle Molly worried about the stress the approaching weekend brought her.

Jess told her to "screw 'em and get out and get free!"

Out of all of them, Jess had always been the rebel.

And then her cell rang. She checked Caller ID. Jessica.

Alexa answered. "Jess. Did you find the records?"

Her cheerful friend spoke in a hushed voice. "Got 'em. Had to wait until the Big Bad Alpha was out running with his mate to use his PC. My internet connection sucks. They blocked me from most sites last month after I put my adopted brother's photo on an internet site for gay men. No one ever has a sense of humor around here."

Amusement filled her. Jess was forever playing jokes on her family, mainly because they weren't "my real family." Jessica had been adopted and still searched for her birth parents.

"I took the information you gave me on the Double B ranch and plugged it into the Lupine business database. Every alpha of every Lupine pack has to register his business with the database so there's a file on them. Best of all, they have to file a photo, too. I'm emailing you the file I downloaded. I wanted to dig deeper into the database, but didn't have time."

"Won't you get in trouble?"

"Naw. Erased my history. Big Bad Alpha is so egotistical, he won't even suspect." Jessica's voice dropped. "You okay, Alexa? You need help?"

Alexa's fingers gripped the phone. "I'll be fine. Don't worry about me. You have your hands full with your family."

"Oh, I keep them on their toes. You hang in there, 'kay? Love you!"

"Love you, too."

She hung up and headed for her laptop. Alexa clicked on the email from Jessica and held her breath as the file downloaded.

She read through the text. Registered owner and authorized to conduct business: Jeremiah Taylor.

Then she looked at the photo.

Her blood pressure plummeted. Sweet goddess.

Raphael stared out from the computer screen, arrogant and cold as ever, his dark gaze hinting of secrets.

Alexa had no appetite for lunch. The tray Jane brought over remained untouched. Instead, she tried to concentrate on the work J.J. had asked her to complete.

Mid-afternoon, J.J. stopped by as she sat on the back porch. Faded jeans accented his long legs and tight butt, and his gray T-shirt molded to his strong biceps and muscled chest. Her breath hitched a little. J.J. was so sexy and hot.

Maybe she'd keep an image of him in her mind Sunday night when she went to "Raphael's" bed.

He handed her a small white box. She opened it and withdrew a quartz crystal swinging from a silver chain. The stone was polished and bright.

"Put it on. It contains a very powerful, ancient spell. It will protect you against anything bad happening to you, whether it's me, Raphael or the Easter Bunny. No more bad magick."

"There is no such thing as the Easter Bunny."

He grinned, showing a flash of even, white teeth. "True. I ate him long ago."

Alexa laughed, glad he'd broken the tension. She held the crystal to the light, admiring the way the colors split into rainbows. "Where did you get it?"

"I bought it from an elderly witch in town."

"It must have cost a fortune."

"You're worth it."

He fastened the clasp around her neck. The crystal lay against her skin, warm and comforting, but not as much as his concern.

They sat with tall glasses of cool lemonade on the balcony. J.J. told her how much help she'd provided through her financial analysis of the ranch's trail rides.

"Good idea to offer half-price rides on the new, shorter trail and then a tour of the ranch. I like the way you think, Alexa. Encourage them to stay longer and they'll purchase more." He leaned back in the rocking chair and drank, his tanned throat muscles working.

Warmth spread through her body, and not only from his praise. Why did her heart beat so much faster whenever he was near? Soon, she'd have to leave him. Her family's needs, and getting them away from Daniel's pack, came first.

"After Sunday, you'll be gone," he said, as if reading her thoughts. "Unless you'd care to stick around."

She swallowed past the lump in her throat. "I'd like that. Very much. But it's impossible."

"I want you in my life, Alexa. I want you so much I feel like I'd die if you said no." He set down his glass of lemonade and squeezed her hand. "But I won't hold you back if you truly desire to leave."

"My family…"

"Bring them here to the ranch to live. There's plenty of space."

"Taylor won't allow it. And how could you be in my life after I sleep with Taylor? Would you really want me after that?"

"How could you assume I wouldn't want you? I told you, Alexa, I want you very much after Sunday night."

She pushed her hand through her hair, and sighed.

"Why do you do that?" he asked suddenly. "With your hair?"

"This?" She repeated the gesture.

At his nod, she felt her face heat.

"Alexa," he prodded. "Tell me. Is it because you're nervous around me? Or are you hiding something?"

Now the heat spread throughout her body. "It's, ah, a little embarrassing. Something stupid I did in college."

"I won't laugh at you. I'd never do that."

Alexa fiddled with her water glass, tracing a bead of

condensation down the smooth surface. "It was my freshman year in college. There was this guy I really liked. But he had his eye on this other girl. I used to watch her, thought if I could mimic her gestures because she was so... human...maybe I'd catch his eye. I found out that Skin women play with their hair a lot to draw attention to their face, get a guy's interest."

Now J.J. leaned forward. "Go on."

"So I started running my hand through my hair, looking away. It didn't work. After that, I guess I kept doing that gesture to remind myself that even when things get rough, I can have control of the situation." She ducked her head. "I also do it when I'm around a guy I find.... very sexy."

Alexa stared at him and blurted out the truth. "I do it around you because I want you so badly, J.J. And when I'm forced to go to Taylor's bed Sunday, I'll close my eyes and think of you."

His eyes widened. "You feel it, too, what's between us. It's more than desire. It's the spark between two Lupines who are meant to be mated."

"I wish we could," she whispered. "But can we ever be more than friends?"

J.J. reached over and cupped her cheek, his hand warm and rough. "*Yes.* I don't want to be friends with you, *cariño*. I want to be your lover for life. Leave your pack and join with me, here, as my mate. I want a relationship with you that is emotional and intimate. It's what I've longed for my entire life, to have someone as special as you as my partner for life."

Stunned, she nearly dropped the glass. Alexa set it down. "Jeremiah Taylor might voice a protest if he doesn't get his money's worth."

"Take a chance on me," he urged.

Her heart cried out yes. But her mind knew if she broke her bargain, Taylor would inform her alpha and Daniel would wreck her family's lives.

Always the responsible one, the one who bore the brunt of the burden. She must go through with this.

"I want to, but I can't. I signed a contract, and a deal is a deal."

He closed his eyes. "I can wait until after Sunday night when you've honored your contract."

"And then would you want me after I slept with Taylor? After I sold myself...like a whore?"

Tears rose in her throat and she struggled to control them. *Think of happier times, don't cry, don't cry....*

"It's not like that," he protested. "I'd never think of you like that. Don't you dare call yourself that word."

Now the tears filled her eyes. "It's true. I'm doing this for my family. A good enough reason, but the result is still the same. I need to be alone for a while. Excuse me."

Alexa left the porch and went inside, heading for the bathroom and slamming the door shut. The tears flowed as she bent over the sink, running water to disguise the sound of her sobs. No one ever saw her cry.

No one.

After a few minutes, she went outside, but J.J. was gone. Probably he'd left in disappointment after her rejection.

What a ripe mess. She'd finally found a guy she longed to mate with, only she couldn't have him.

She had no illusions about her future lover. Raphael was Taylor, and she had proof.

For the next few hours, she sat on the balcony, trying to read. A cooling breeze from the rushing river teased her hair.

She smelled a strong aroma of citrus mixed with spices and sensed Raphael's presence as he slid from the shadows.

"Miss Grant?" Raphael stood nearby. His dark gaze regarded her, secrets hidden within. Her stomach roiled with anxiety.

I know who you really are. Bastard.

"Mr. Taylor requests you join him in the library in the main house in half an hour."

What a pile of horse crap. Did he really think she was so stupid that she wouldn't see through his ruse? Alexa set down the book and decided to play along. "*The* Jeremiah Taylor? The male who purchased me for one night? I was beginning to think he was an illusion. A cowardly one."

His mouth quirked slightly. "He is no illusion. He is very much real, and wishes you to join him. And he is far from a coward." Raphael handed her a folded note. "His instructions are within."

When he left, she read the note. The handwriting was crisp and authoritative, written in an elegant script. "I wish to demonstrate a preview of Sunday night. When you arrive at the house, go to the dining room. There is a robe draped over a chair. Undress down to your panties and put on the robe. There should be nothing between you and the robe but skin. J. Taylor."

A shiver raced through her. A preview of what? What he'd be like in bed?

Finally she would meet the elusive Jeremiah Taylor. She knew this was coming, knew the wolf wanted to meet her, sample his prey before dining fully Sunday night.

As she made her way to the main house, Alexa scrubbed her sweating palms.

No one was in the house. The grandfather clocked ticked away the minutes as she undressed and put on the lovely Chinese red silk robe. Alexa left her clothing folded neatly on the chair and climbed the stairs to the last door on the left.

She opened the door.

Shades and drapes were drawn tight against the setting sun. Only a fire flickering dimly in the stone hearth provided ambient light, casting flickering shadows around the room. A Chinese screen sat in one corner. Threads of smoke from sandalwood incense snaked through the air.

"Miss Grant. A pleasure. I am Jeremiah Jackson Taylor."

The low, rough voice from behind the screen sounded vaguely familiar. But it sounded tinny, as if he were trying to disguise his true voice. With the incense, she also couldn't discern the male's true scent. Her Lupine senses seemed muddied.

Whoever spoke wished to remain a mystery.

"Please remove your robe and leave your upper body bared. I would like to see you. And soothe your fears."

Alexa dropped the robe and shivered, suddenly cold. *I can't do this. I can't.*

"Close your eyes."

She felt something smooth and silky slide over her

116

eyes, and tie in the back. "Too tight?" the husky voice asked.

She shook her head. "I want to see you." *See your face, Raphael, confirm my worst fears…*

"In time."

She shuddered as two hands stroked her breasts almost lazily, calloused thumbs flicking over her nipples. It felt wonderful. Her body betrayed her as her nipples turned hard.

The only way she could endure would be to imagine someone else. And then deep inside, she pulled on all her wolf instincts and thought of J.J. His deep voice rumbling in her ear, his sexy scent and hard body.

Her imagination conjured the cowboy, and pushed all else aside.

His hands kept stroking her, creating a delightful friction. Odd.

"What is odd?"

Alexa hadn't realized she'd spoken aloud. "You don't have smooth hands. For a reclusive millionaire, your hands are rough."

A deep chuckle. "Billionaire," he corrected. "I work hard on my ranch, along with my cowboys."

A light pinch, squeeze. Alexa shuddered.

"Did I hurt you?" the deep voice inquired.

"N-no."

"Did you find pleasure in what I did?"

Damn she would not give him the satisfaction. This was sex, nothing more. Just get on with it, she silently implored.

He lightly pinched again, wringing a tiny moan from her.

"Tell me. Do you find pleasure in that?"

Alexa made a low humming sound deep in her throat. He gently pushed her downward, guiding her hands to the desktop. The crystal swung gently between her breasts.

"Face the desk. Place your palms flat on the desk, lean over and spread your legs."

Shaking, she did as he asked.

"Wider, Miss Grant."

"Why?" she blurted out.

A deep chuckle. "I wish to see if your lovely little pussy is wet for me."

The words sent a fresh wave of arousal pulsing through her. Anger surfaced at her body's betrayal. But she obeyed and widened her stance.

Then his hands reached around her waist, trailed down her bare torso, sliding possessively over the slight rise of her belly, down her panties. He edged a finger along the pretty lace waistband. Alexa bit her lip, struggling not to react.

He slid a hand into her panties, between her legs.

"Excellent. You are quite soaked and ready for my cock. Can you imagine my cock at your entrance as I nudge it forward, preparing to enter you?"

Alexa's nails dug at the desk. "They say it hurts. I doubt I'll enjoy it."

"The first time can be difficult for a virgin. But there is pleasure as well. Such as this."

His forefinger parted her slick folds and stroked across her soaked slit. This time Alexa moaned.

"Do you find pleasure in what I do?"

"Please…"

He thrust his finger gently into her tight channel while his thumb lazily stroked against the tiny nub at

SEDUCTION

her clit, slow, deliberate swirls as if they had all the time in the world. "Tell me, Miss Grant. I have no desire to hurt you or make your first time painful. Do you enjoy this?"

Alexa grabbed the desktop and opened her legs wider. "Yes!"

A deep chuckle. His finger thrust gently in and out of her vagina. "Good."

She moaned.

"Imagine me fucking you, Alexa. My cock is stroking deep inside you, my hands are upon your breasts, my tongue in your mouth. I am claiming you so fully you wish to scream with the pleasure, not the pain. You feel me deep within your body as I thrust, my body hotly sliding over yours, pressing you down. You try to resist the pleasure I am giving you, but it is futile. Give in, Alexa. You want to scream with it. Let me hear you scream."

"No," she wailed.

He stroked harder, creating an exquisite pressure. "Yes," he murmured.

She must not give in. Never. But the erotic friction continued, and her body tensed, poised on the edge of climax. She couldn't help it...

"Yes, come for me, my sweet Alexa, come for me."

This was not the cold, cruel joining she'd imagined in her dreams, but a maelstrom of desire so intense, she wanted to faint. The bastard was seducing her with his wicked hands, stroking her to a passion she did not want to feel.

Biting back a scream, she gripped the desk's edge as the pleasure swirled. Oh gods, she needed this, wanted this badly. Wanted him deep inside her, thrusting so

119

hard that the desk shook. Wanted him filling her, regardless of the fact that he was a heartless billionaire and a total stranger.

She clenched hard around the pressure of his invading finger and then sensation exploded in her loins. Alexa cried out J.J's name. His name on her lips, his face in her mind.

If only he could be J.J.

She expected Taylor to be smug, chuckle or make some arrogant remark as she collapsed to the desktop, her limbs quivering madly. Instead there was only the barest deep sigh as he withdrew his hand from her body. He lightly pinched her buttocks.

"You may see yourself out."

The voice sounded disembodied and emotionless, as if her orgasm meant little to him. Shame filled her, pushing aside the erotic bliss. Alexa let her anger rise again. The hell with shame. She should kick him in the balls.

Alexa tore off her blindfold, but she was alone in the room. She fumbled for her robe, drew it on and fled the room.

J.J. slid back into the shadows, fighting the compulsion to kiss Alexa senseless, whisper his deepest secret. But she was not ready yet. Hell, he was not ready yet.

She'd called out his name and he'd nearly folded. Her sweet release had made his cock hard as stone, had nearly shattered his resolve.

Not yet. But soon. First, he must be absolutely

certain of trusting her. And he could not do that until he knew she became submissive to his will, not Daniel's.

Leaning against the wall, he removed the mouthpiece that disguised his voice and then slowly licked her juices from his soaked fingers. His cock throbbed painfully in his jeans. He could no longer stand it.

Leaning against the bookcase, he unzipped his jeans, the sound harsh in the quiet library. He seized his cock, pressed a towel against the overly sensitive head, and began to stroke. Imagining he was thrusting hard and heavy into Alexa, her face sweet with hot passion, her dark gaze filled with wonder as he claimed her in the flesh, making her his. Feeling her clench around him as she climaxed, her cries echoing his as he emptied his seed deep inside her...

J.J. groaned as his cock spurted hotly into the towel, his body shuddering as he came, wishing it were the real thing, Alexa in his arms for life.

He cleaned himself up and threw the towel into the fire. As he emerged from the library, feigning a coolness he did not feel, Raphael waited for him in the hallway. His beta regarded him with his deep, dark gaze.

No matter how long he'd known Raphael, he never guessed what the male thought.

"And did you enjoy Miss Grant?"

J.J. ground to a halt. "Is it your business if I did?"

They were friends, but Raphael always held part of himself aloof.

"No, it is not. But as your friend, I advise you to let go of this charade and take a leap of trust." Raphael leaned against the wall. "You both care for each other. The air practically crackles with sex when both of you are together. Why continue like this?"

"I have my reasons." And Raphael didn't need to know them. "Did you find out anything from the new security cameras?"

Raphael frowned. "Nothing, except the usual comings and goings."

J.J. squeezed his fists. "When I find the guy who's doing this, I'll take him apart."

"Perhaps you are not the only one who is masquerading. Have you considered that whomever's infiltrated the ranch, it's someone who hates you more than he loves money?"

"Daniel?" J.J. shook his head. "I'd know his scent, would know that bastard from a mile away."

"Unless he hired someone to do his dirty work." He gave J.J. a speculative look. "Or conspired with someone who is already here."

Alexa. No, it couldn't be her. He could not believe it. J.J. rubbed the back of his neck. "Are the other pack members back yet?

At Raphael's nod, he continued. "Double the security detail. Cancel the trail rides for the next few days. No tourists on the ranch. Family illness. Refund their money and give them vouchers. No one gets in or out without your permission."

"And Miss Grant? Do you wish me to guard her?"

"No." The word came out more sharply than he'd intended. "I have a list of things I need you to get in town. I'll stay with her. But Alexa may want a few things in town, too."

Raphael's mouth quirked in an amused smile. "Of

course. Jane has a shopping list as well. I am more than happy to be everyone's ground hog."

"Huh?"

The beta's smile slipped. "Do I have my animals confused again?"

J.J. raised his brows. "Go-pher." He shook his head.

"Ah, yes. Another burrowing rodent. I shall stop by the guest house and inquire if Miss Grant needs anything."

His beta followed him into J.J.'s office and wrote down the list J.J. dictated, then folded the note and put it into his pocket.

J.J. watched him leave, deeply troubled. Someone was playing games with him. He trusted Rafe utterly, but what about Jane? Did his housekeeper disapprove of Alexa and showed that disapproval by these incidents?

Nonsense. Jane and others in his pack were loyal.

Something else was threading discord and suspicion between himself and Alexa. Something very powerful with strong, dark magick.

But in the meantime, he must find a way to free Alexa from her pack. He trusted Daniel no more than she did.

He sat at his desk, opened the bottom drawer and pulled out a thick book of ancient Lupine laws.

When he'd formed his own pack years ago, Tristan, the Silver Wizard, presented the book to him as a gift. Every alpha heading a pack possessed one. He'd tucked the tome away, never expecting to crack it open.

J.J. opened to the first page and began to read.

Alexa had never showered so quickly. Her hands shaking badly, she poured rose-scented shower gel onto a washcloth and scrubbed her body so fiercely her skin turned red.

Heated embarrassment flowed through her veins, erasing the sensual pleasure. With only his hands and his husky whispers, the mysterious Jeremiah Taylor had turned her from stoic to sobbing and pleading for release.

She'd long suspected her sensual nature would surface with the right male. But the *wrong* male had coaxed out every ounce of it today. And then dismissed her like the whore she'd become. Well, she was selling herself to him, after all.

Anger and self-disgust filled her. Alexa scrubbed herself harder, wishing she could rid her body of the lingering memory of his hands touching her.

Shutting off the water, she stepped out of the shower, dried off and dressed in black trousers, a long-sleeved gray blouse and knotted her hair into a tight bun.

Alexa studied her reflected in the dresser mirror. She looked utterly unsexy and unappealing. And she smelled like a rose garden.

Good.

Barely had she plopped onto the chair by the fireplace when someone knocked at the door. Oh goddess, was this Raphael—Taylor, she corrected herself—standing outside with a knowing smirk, wanting to know how she'd enjoyed his attentions?

When she opened the door, it was indeed Raphael outside. Dressed in a black T-shirt, jeans and a black leather jacket, he looked like a biker. Still dangerous, but with the air of courtesy that always masked him.

Alexa glared at him, silently daring him to taunt her, but he merely nodded.

"I am headed into town to pick up a few items. Do you require anything?"

How about a chastity belt made of steel? "Thanks, I'm fine. No, wait."

The rose-scented gel certainly did mask her scent. Maybe it would turn him off.

Raphael—Taylor—whatever his name was! unfolded a sheet of paper. "Do you have a pen so I can write down the items?"

Alexa led the hateful bastard over to the small desk by the French windows and handed him a pen. He set the paper down and wrote down what she told him. *Rose-scented bath oil. Rose-scented shower gel. Rose-scented body lotion.*

"Do you possess an affinity for flowers, Miss Grant, or are you wishing to cloak your true scent?"

She narrowed her eyes. "What does it matter to you? If I wish to bathe in cod liver oil, it's none of your business."

When she looked at Raphael, his expression remained inscrutable. He folded the note and placed it into his jacket pocket. At the door he paused and turned, his dark gaze shuttered.

"Know this, Miss Grant. Things are not always as they seem. Mr. Jeremiah Taylor is not as you think. He is not even who you think he is."

Alexa narrowed her eyes. "You playing games with me? Because I don't play games and when I'm forced into it, I always win because I don't care about breaking rules."

125

He arched a dark brow. "I only wish to convey the truth. Mr. Taylor is someone who very much cares for you. You can trust me on this."

"Right," she said scathingly. "Because the way *Mr. Taylor* treated me was so very respectful."

"You didn't enjoy it?"

"Get out!" She somehow forced the words past her humiliation. "I can't trust anyone," she said, "least of all you."

CHAPTER 8

Friday afternoon, J.J. galloped on his horse toward the river, needing this release, needing fresh air. He and Raphael had trails to ride through and examine for potholes. Every day, he'd made it a habit of personally checking each trail every afternoon for possible problems.

Dust flew up beneath his horses' hooves. He relished the thundering of the beast, how his own heart pounded in response. This was living, wild and free where no Skin and no Lupine ruled over him.

"J.J.!"

He ground to a halt and spun his mount around as Raphael rode up, and pulled up short. Rafe tipped back his black Stetson. "Your future mate has company. Jane radioed me that a Jessica Tyrell, who calls herself Miss Grant's best friend, just pulled up to the gate in a taxi and demanded to see her. Jane told her to leave, but Jessica said she'd sit with the meter running all day until she was allowed inside. That one is a quite a minx."

Though Raphael's expression remained carefully blank, J.J. sensed the beta's increased heartbeat. He was

127

interested in this new arrival. He would not deny Alexa her friend, and he was curious to see the female who made Raphael react so.

J.J. pulled free the radio from the casing on his belt and told Jane to send away the taxi, but keep the woman waiting until he arrived. He replaced the radio and told Rafe, "Ride back with me to the house."

When they reached the main house parking lot, the woman stood, suitcase in hand, by the front entrance, Jane guarding her with a wary look.

Raphael and J.J. exchanged glances. With her waist-length, corkscrew-red curls, snapping gray eyes and stubborn set to her chin, Alexa's friend could be trouble. But he knew Alexa needed someone to help her sort through her emotions.

"Miss Jessica Tyrell? I'm J.J. Garcia, foreman of the ranch. This is Raphael Amador, Mr. Taylor's beta. Welcome to the Double B."

Jessica studied him, then her bold gaze swung over to Raphael, who'd suddenly gone still as if his wolf scented something interesting.

Very interesting.

"Hi. If you don't mind, I need to see my friend Alexa. You two can go back to playing John Wayne."

"Jane, will you show Miss Tyrell to the guest house and find a room for her?"

Jane nodded. Tossing back her long red curls, Jessica followed the housekeeper to the guest house.

Raphael kept staring after her. "That one, her hair... I have seen only one other Lupine with that color hair. She..."

"Is trouble." J.J. dug his heels into his horse's sides. "Come on, pardner, we have a trail to inspect."

128

Alexa laughed and hugged Jessica for the third time since her friend had lugged her suitcase into a spare guest room the housekeeper found for her.

"I can't believe you booked a plane ticket and came here for me!"

"I couldn't let you go through this alone. Friends for life, forever." She fist-bumped Alexa, and her cheerful grin made Alexa smile. "I have to leave Sunday. Wish I could stay until Monday, but I can't."

"I'm so glad you're here." She hugged her friend again. As Jess unpacked, she sat on the bed, telling her about the ranch and J.J.

"I really like him, Jess." Alexa bit her lip. "I think I've fallen in love with him."

Jessica turned from the bureau, a fistful of purple silk panties in hand. Alexa noted with a smile that Jess still liked wearing her days of the week underwear. In college, Skins called them fat. Like her, Jessica had wide hips, big breasts and a butt, but her friend had flaunted these assets and had a love for silk lingerie.

"Good for you. About time you fell in love and did something for yourself."

"He asked me to mate him." She sighed. "But I have to go through with this. I'm obligated."

"Screw obligations. Run away with him!"

"My family…"

"They'll survive."

"I can't take that chance, not with Daniel. Every month he gets a little more… crazy."

Jess flopped onto the bed on her stomach and sighed. "I know. I'd give anything to get you out of there. My alpha is just as strict. He and my foster parents always keep watch over me. I can never have fun."

"How did you get permission to leave?"

"Made a deal with my foster monster. Told her if I could get the weekend away to visit you, I'd iron all the family's clothing for the next four weeks."

"Jess! You hate ironing."

She shrugged. "I wasn't going to abandon you, not now when you need me. But I have to leave Sunday afternoon. Molly was going to fly up here as well, but she couldn't get the money together for the flight. She said you need anything, call."

Overwhelmed with her friends' support, Alexa swallowed past a lump in her throat. "Thanks."

"I just wish I could stay, but I can't. The only way my alpha gave me the cash to fly out here was a promise I'd babysit for him Sunday night."

She was so lucky to have such good, loyal friends.

"So what's your plan for Sunday night?" Jessica asked.

"I thought I'd disguise my true scent. Maybe he won't be as... vigorous if he doesn't scent me as a female Lupine." She pointed to the desk. Jessica bounded off the bed and examined the items Raphael had purchased in town.

"Rose scented lotion?" Jessica uncapped the lid and sniffed. "No male Lupine will be distracted if you smother yourself in this. It's like dousing a forest fire with a cup of water. And it will clog your own senses when you go to Taylor's bed. If he tries to disguise his real identity, your nostrils will be too filled with roses to detect his scent."

"Good point. I didn't think that through."

"Because you're too tense, trying to deal with too much. That's why I'm here." Jess squeezed her hand. "Anything I can do to help."

"I need to relax."

Jess gave a crooked grin. "Lots of cute cowboys around here. Let's go outside and watch the scenery. It is very peaceful. I could do with a little peace and quiet."

The housekeeper had left a bowl of fresh peaches on the porch, along with a pitcher of iced tea. Alexa poured them both glasses. Jessica selected a peach and sniffed it.

"Fresh fruit! What a luxury. I adore peaches." She bit into it with a happy sigh.

They watched the cowboys return from the trail. Alexa pointed out J.J., riding a big, black stallion. Raphael was mounted on a chestnut.

"J.J. is so sexy on a horse," Alexa told her.

"He's very cute. But the other one, that Raphael." Jess shivered. "He looked at me like he knows what I look like naked. He's dangerous, Alexa. I wish he wasn't your mysterious billionaire."

"Me too."

Alexa picked up her glass and watched J.J. gallop toward the barn. Raphael dismounted and tethered his horse to a railing near the guest house.

Jessica fished her cell phone from her pocket, checked her messages.

"Nothing. No whining boss, no foster monster wanting me to run to the grocery store, no young asking me to shift into wolf so they can dress me in dog costumes. Free at last, for a few days." She tossed the phone up into the air. Raphael reached out, grabbed it in mid-air.

"Hey, give that back!" Jessica sprang out of her chair.

He palmed the phone. "Is 'please' not in your vocabulary?"

"Nope, but 'screw you' is."

"Is that an invitation?" he asked politely.

"Only if you wish me to claw your face. Now give me back my damn phone!"

"You need to learn restraint, Miss Tyrell. Has no one ever taught you to rein in your impulses?" Raphael asked.

"No one dares try. You wanna volunteer?" Jessica challenged.

Alexa choked on her sip of tea.

"You should be more careful with expressing your desires, Miss Tyrell, or they may come true," he said softly, placing her phone on the table. "I came here to inform you that dinner will be served at the main house at six o'clock. Both of you are expected to attend."

Oh boy. Jess, more than sweet-tempered Molly, hated being ordered around. Jessica glared at Raphael. "We are?"

"I expect you will arrive, dressed and presentable. We have rules on this ranch and visitors are required to obey them."

Jessica gave a smile that did not meet her eyes. "I expect you'll have to get used to disappointment."

She picked up her peach and took a large bite. Juice dripped down her chin, onto her chest. Fascinated, Alexa watched her friend lick the fruit in slow, deliberate strokes, watched Raphael's pupils dilate and his breathing quicken. He fisted his hands.

The wolf was getting very turned on. In fact, he

seemed much more interested in Jess than in Alexa.

"You will be at the main house at six," Raphael ordered, but he spoke to Jessica, his voice tight.

Jessica set down the fruit on the table and licked her mouth. Raphael's gaze tracked every move.

"I'm taking my girl here out for dinner, get her a change of scenery."

"No one is allowed to enter or leave the ranch without permission." Raphael narrowed his gaze.

"Permission from whom? Jeremiah Taylor? Soon as he shows his face, I'll listen. Until then, I'll grant us permission. You can dine without us."

"Jess," Alexa warned.

"What?" Jessica spread out her hands. "It's not as if he can do anything to me."

Raphael gave her friend a long, thoughtful look, then walked away.

CHAPTER 9

As promised, Jessica took her out to dinner in nearby Durango. They drove Alexa's rental to town and found an Irish bar. As they laughed and talked over old times while eating burgers, Alexa noticed J.J. and Raphael at a nearby table.

Far enough away not to eavesdrop, but still close enough for her to be aware they were watching her.

Guarding her, it seemed. After the treadmill incident, she felt reassured by J.J.'s presence. Once or twice she glanced up to see Raphael staring at Jessica.

She poked her friend in the arm. "He likes you."

Glancing over her shoulder, Jessica smiled. "Want me to take your place Sunday night? That would shock him. Especially when he finds out I'm a real redhead."

Alexa wanted to smile, but emotion clogged her throat. "I just wish it would be J.J. I always wanted my first time to be special, not like this."

With an angry fist, she wiped her eyes, refusing to cry. "And look at me, getting all emotional. I swore I'd never break down in front of anyone."

"I'm not anyone, Alexa. It's me. And remember how I bawled in front of you like a baby during graduation because everyone else had family there, so proud of them, and I had no one? If it wasn't for you and your family and Molly and her parents, I would have been all alone."

Jessica squeezed her hand. "Oh honey, it's going to be okay. Just close your eyes and think of J.J. doing it. And you'll be free from Daniel. Your family is lucky to have you care so much for them."

She squeezed back. "I'm the lucky one, to have friends like you and Molly."

"It's the three of us together, always. Remember? We're not going to let those Skins get under our fur. It's going to be okay. Everything's going to be okay."

Her friend gave an impish grin, scrolled through her phone, selected an app. Music blared over the cell. Swaying in her chair, Jessica began singing David Guetta's "Sexy Bitch."

Alexa smiled. "You're going to get us tossed out."

"Then I won't do the 'dance.' But come on Alexa! This is our song. We are big, bad sexy bitches and you know those guys secretly want us." Jessica winked.

Alexa sang along. In school, it had been their traditional way of thumbing their noses at the world. Friday nights in their apartment, a tub of chocolate ice cream, music blaring on the stereo and singing and dancing "their" theme song. Every time one of them got depressed, missing other Lupines, the others forced her to sing and do the "dance."

Damn they were big, bad sexy bitches. Sexy female werewolves Skins mocked for being chubby, when all the time they could tear those boys apart with fangs and claws.

At a nearby table, two men stared at them with

disapproving expressions. Jessica jumped up from her chair and wriggled her bottom. "Look at this boootah!"

Howling with laughter, Alexa shook her head. Jess was right. It would be okay. Everything would be okay.

With Jessica visiting, the weekend sped by. They rode along the trails, with J.J. leading them in front and Raphael guarding their rear. The following night, she and Jessica ate with the pack's cowboys in the mess hall of the bunkhouse. Raphael and J.J. joined them. The cowboys enjoyed Jessica's jokes, while Raphael kept staring as if trying to figure Jessica out.

No one could figure out Jess.

On Saturday night, as Jessica kept everyone entertained at dinner, J.J. remained by Alexa's side. He kept reaching for her hand, but she quietly drew back, not wanting to draw attention to herself.

Besides, it was too painful, knowing Raphael would be her first lover, not J.J.

"Walk outside with me," he urged.

When she hesitated, he pulled her to her feet and tugged her out the door. Alexa walked with him along the dimly lit pathway leading to the barn. The moon shone overhead, a lemon wedge in the starlit sky. It was so lovely here, so peaceful. Nothing like the constant tension at Daniel's pack.

How she'd hate leaving this ranch behind.

J.J. stopped and turned toward her, his hands cupping her face. "Alexa, I have something I must say to you. You have such a gentle heart. You're always thinking of others, putting your family before your own

136

needs. It's time you reached out for what you desire, instead of what you think is right."

His thumbs gently stroked over her cheeks. Alexa leaned into his touch. "I want to," she confessed. "But how can I take what I want the most, when it all will vanish by Monday morning?"

Beneath the moonlight, she saw his smile. "Have a little faith, *cariño*. If you can't have faith in fate, then have faith in me."

His kiss felt so sweet and tender, she wanted to cling to him and melt into his arms. But then lights snapped on outside, and several pack members came out, laughing and joking.

J.J. drew back, but kept cupping her face with his hands.

"You'd better let me go before someone sees us and complains."

A cowboy glanced at them and J.J. growled at him. "Leave us, now."

The Lupine scuttled off into the shadows.

"Was that necessary? I don't want to get you into trouble. He could report you."

J.J. leaned his forehead against hers. "That was my Jeremiah side coming out."

"Your Jeremiah side. You keep saying that. Does everyone have one? Is everyone on this ranch as alpha as THE alpha?"

A low growl rumbled in his throat and he stepped back. "There's only one alpha in this pack. Alexa, don't you realize this by now?"

For a wild moment she hoped she'd been wrong and Jessica had been wrong, too. Hoped Raphael was not the alpha, but J.J. was.

Then she remembered her friend's expert hacking ability and her spirits sank.

"I realize I have tonight before I have to pay the price. So come back inside with me into the bright lights and let's not think about Sunday."

J.J. said nothing, but steered her inside, his hand at the small of her back.

As they sat around the fire with the other Lupines, laughing and swapping stories, Alexa tried not to think of this night ending. But tomorrow night would arrive all too soon.

A taxi shuttled Jessica away early Sunday afternoon, whisking her to the airport. Alexa spent the rest of the day trying to occupy herself.

She'd dined alone at the main house. Jane told her J.J. was out running errands. As Alexa ate, she wondered if he forced himself to stay away from her, knowing what would transpire later that night.

Someone knocked on her door after dinner. When she opened it, no one was in the hall. But a note sat on the floor.

As Alexa read the note, a chill raced down her spine. The same, crisp, flowing handwriting instructed her to shower, dress and arrive at the main house by 8 p.m. to fulfill her contract. She was to remove her crystal when she undressed.

So cold.

Passionless.

Lights illuminated the flagstone pathway to the main house. Alexa's heart sank to her stomach as she thought of what awaited her. She'd survive. And tomorrow, she and her family would be free as soon as Daniel received the wire transfer.

And what of J.J.? He'd asked her to stay. But it wasn't his call. Not his ranch.

She thought of Raphael awaiting her in Jeremiah's bedroom. Raphael with his cold, dark eyes and hardness and slight cruel twist to his sensual mouth.

You can face anything, get through anything. It's only one night. Just close your eyes and pretend.

She went to the living room as the note had instructed. Draped over the sofa's back was a red silk robe. Shivering, she undressed, folding her clothing neatly and placing it on the sofa with her protective crystal, and donned the robe.

As instructed, she went upstairs to the last room on the right.

Shadows danced on the wallpaper, cast by the flickering fire in the hearth. The room smelled of sage and incense. An enormous four-poster bed, the sheets neatly turned down, dominated the bedroom.

Alexa bit her lip, removed the robe.

She climbed onto the enormous bed. Her heart hammered against her chest as a man stepped from behind the Chinese screen, quietly studying her. He was clad in shadow.

A bit afraid, Alexa trembled. The man approached the bed, silent as mist. He leaned a hip on the bed's edge and ran a caressing hand over her trembling body.

"You're mine, sweet Alexa. I could not allow another male to claim you. I refuse to allow another male to have you."

Then he went to the bedside lamp and snapped it on.

139

Confused, she sat up on the bed and stared, her mouth wobbling.

"I don't understand."

J.J. stood before her in an ankle-length robe of burgundy. A hank of inky black hair spilled across his forehead. He looked dark and dangerous, and very sexy.

Never had she seen him like this before, as if he'd transformed from the laid-back cowboy to a powerful alpha capable of snapping someone's neck in half.

Climbing out of bed, Alexa faced him and lifted her chin. "Where is Jeremiah Taylor?"

"You still don't get it?"

"No and you'd better get out before Taylor gets here!" A lump clogged her throat. "You shouldn't be here, but I'm glad you are. I want you so much. I want you so badly that I'm almost willing to forgo my promise to Jeremiah Taylor."

J.J. stalked forward, furious and impassioned, his blue eyes glittering like dark sapphires. She had never seen him this intense and she wanted to back away, but her heart beat faster and her body thrilled at his nearness.

"The hell with Jeremiah Jackson fucking Taylor! I don't care about him anymore. Gods be damned, I fucking love you!"

He fisted a hand in her hair, and kissed her, his mouth hard and authoritative. He kissed her as if he'd never see her again. He kissed her as if all his previous, gentle kisses had been as much of an illusion as the man himself.

Alexa sagged against him, helpless against this

maelstrom of passion. His mouth turned coaxing and soft as he nibbled against her lips, leading her into a seductive dance she could not resist.

Nor did she want to.

Later, she would deal with the consequences, the questions. For now all she wanted was this male in her arms, his body inside her, claiming what had been his all along.

He sampled her mouth, running his tongue along the generous curve of her lips. Alexa clung to his shoulders as his tongue thrust past her lips. Her mouth opened under the subtle, demanding pressure of his. Desire suffused her and she drew closer.

With an impatient shrug, he divested himself of the robe, letting it spill to the floor. Thick, wavy hair black as midnight spilled over his forehead. Alexa felt a sudden sexual response as she imagined tunneling her fingers through the wavy locks as he pleasured her with his mouth.

Alexa stared in fascination at his thick, erect penis. "Why did you have me remove the crystal?"

"It blurs the senses, blinds you to the truth. I need you to see me, Alexa, see me as I really am." He framed her face with his hands and then kissed her.

When she parted her lips, he fisted a hand in her hair, tipped her head back and ravaged her mouth. He kissed her as if he would die if he didn't claim her body. His tongue stroked deep, as he would soon stroke deep inside her body.

Alexa ran her palms over him, feeling the twin muscles that divided his back, the smooth firmness of his ass, the strength in his limbs, the power in his arms. She craved him like a drug, needed all his male hardness pressing into her, making her his own. Her wolf howled for him to take her, the sexual craving intensifying until it burned like living flame.

Still kissing, they tumbled into the bed. Then J.J. rolled off her, reached into the nightstand and removed a tube of lubricant. He squirted a small portion onto his palms, rubbed his hands together.

Very gently, he laid his palms against the slight rise of her abdomen. Alexa jerked back.

"Shhh," he soothed.

"What is this?"

"Massage oil." J.J. bent down and licked a dollop off her belly. "I know your first time will be painful, Alexa, and I plan to make it as enjoyable as possible. I want you to feel pleasure."

He rubbed circles over her abdomen, working his way up to her breasts. Every stroke of his rough hands aroused her, making her hot and wet between her legs. Alexa closed her eyes and moaned as J.J. palmed her breasts, flicking his oiled thumbs over her nipples. They softened beneath his ministrations, then the peaks crested.

Then he bent his head and took the right one into his mouth.

With expert skill, he ran his tongue over the taut nipple. He suckled her gently, inhaling the fragrance of honey flowing from her core.

J.J. released her nipple. She blinked and wriggled her naked body. He applied more oil to his hands, and returned to her.

"Lie still."

He squeezed her hips and then began long, slow strokes up and down her legs. He paid extra attention to her feet. J.J. ran his oiled hands along the inside of her calves, then up the insides of her splayed thighs.

Then as her skin warmed, he straddled her body.

He kissed her mouth, then dropped tiny, quick kisses over her chin, neck, collarbones, down to her tender breasts. He cupped their heavy weight in his palms, encircling her aching nipples with his thumbs. Enormous heat suffused her body.

Alexa dragged in a deep breath, gripped by such sheer need she couldn't stop what was happening. She'd wanted this badly, wanted him, and he wanted her as much. Caressing him, she felt skin over hard muscle, the soft, springy hairs covering the muscles on his chest. Her hands drifted lower to the pads of muscle ribbing his abdomen. Alexa had dreamed of this moment when she could touch him without abandon or fear. Just the two of them together, locking away the rest of the world and its cares.

She skimmed a hand down his flat, muscled belly and stared with fascination at his long, thick penis. Ridged with veins, it was slightly pointed at the end, but close enough to human so one could not tell the difference. Except when they made love. Alexa shivered with anticipation, remembering the stories about Lupine sex she'd heard from Jessica and Molly.

The wolf's knot, which tied them together and created even more exquisite pleasure for the female. It did not always happen in Skin, especially the first time. And a couple wasn't tied together unless it was a full moon or the female was in heat.

He guided her hand down to his penis. "Touch me," he demanded.

Alexa wrapped her hand around his erection. He was

huge. She grew wetter at the thought of all that male hardness deep inside her.

"You want me." His deep voice rubbed against her in a velvety caress as he pressed a finger against the damp curls at her center. "Deep inside you. Open to me, and let me enter, Alexa. I promise I will do everything to give you sweet pleasure."

Then he once more ravished her mouth, tongue and teeth plundering and claiming. She eagerly kissed him back, opened her mouth wider under his coaxing. J.J. pushed his tongue into the wet cavern of her mouth, mimicking what he would do to her body.

An agony of need twined with eager anticipation as he slid his hands over her naked body. He squeezed hard and broke the kiss. "I love these," he murmured, squeezing her wide hips. "I love every inch of your curves. You're so lush and plumb, the way a woman should be. You've driven me crazy with the need to mate, Alexa. I must have you."

When he pushed her back onto the bed, she held onto his shoulders. J.J. was her anchor as she drowned in a sea of erotic bliss. He cupped her sex, stroked a finger around the edge of her vagina, then parted her with his fingers and pushed a single digit inside. The pleasure was so sharp, she arched and cried out. In and out he stroked, fire licking between her legs. Releasing her grip on him, Alex dug her heels into the mattress.

Tongue and lips worked wicked magick across her skin as he kissed her bare belly, licked the indentation of her navel. Holding onto him, she shivered as he teased and stroked, culling moisture and sliding it across her cleft. He gently rubbed her clit, wringing tiny gasps from her throat. Alexa opened her legs wide in a nameless plea.

"Your mouth tastes like the bite of cold Chardonnay, sweet and succulent. Your skin…" He nuzzled her throat, "tastes like raspberries, but your core…"

She watched him settle between her legs, and then part her thighs. He lowered his head, blew a soft, hot breath against her female flesh and put his mouth on her.

J.J. licked her, his rough tongue stroking her inner folds. His silky hair rubbed against her thighs as he pleasured her, dragging his tongue across her slit.

"You taste like sunshine and fresh air," he murmured against her wet flesh. "Clear water and all my tomorrows. I love tasting you."

Finding her erect clit, he encased it with his mouth. Wildfire blazed through her veins as the delicious pressure began to build, making her bottom clench hard, triggering the instinct to move her hips upward. Alexa grabbed the sheets and fisted them, panting with sharp need, driven by the flicks of his tongue across her engorged nub. She spread her legs open wider, eager for more. Tension built higher as he stroked his tongue faster and harder and then she shattered. Screaming, her body convulsing, she surrendered, sobbing his name.

Bonelessly she sagged against the mattress, panting hard. J.J. sat back and licked his mouth as he studied her.

"I don't know if I can take any more," she gasped, drawing in deep breaths.

He smiled. "You can. And you will."

"And what about you?"

"I will have my pleasure, but not until you've had

more." He gathered her into his arms, and let her recover for a few minutes, murmuring to her in Spanish as he stroked her hair.

Alexa lightly rubbed his erection, coaxing a moan from him. Daringly, she touched the glistening droplets of moisture seeping from the tip of his rigid cock, and then brought them to her mouth. Tasting him, the salt of his pre-cum.

"Now I've tasted you. I have you inside me now," she whispered, licking her mouth.

"And you will have more, much more."

Then his blue eyes glittered with intent. He bent his head to her breast. J.J. licked her hardening nipple very slowly, his flicking tongue making her writhe with pleasure. Then he took it fully into his mouth and suckled deeply.

He caressed her belly, tunneled into the thick, dark curls covering her mound, and slid a finger over her slit. Each stroke made her body taut. A groan rumbled from his deep chest as she undulated her hips against his fingers. Her wolf awakening to the dark sexual magick dancing inside her, Alexa let her claws unsheathe a little, and gently scraped them down his back.

J.J. ceased suckling her nipple and drew backward. "Vixen," he growled.

"Wolf," she corrected, feeling the sensual flush of heat glow inside her. "Don't stop."

Growling softly, he returned to her nipple, as his fingers continued to work wicked magic. Wetness gushed out of her, preparing her to fully take him. Wriggling on the bed, Alexa gasped, her hips jerking up eagerly. He raised his head. Blue eyes the color of sapphire regarded her.

"Let it happen again. I want to watch you cum."

"J.J., please, oh please..."

"I'm making you wet, making you ready to take my cock inside you," he murmured, continuing to caress her flesh. "You like the idea of my big, thick hard cock sliding into your pussy, all nice and tight, feeling me fill you. Making you all hot inside?"

Oh, she needed this badly.

Not ceasing his motions, he sat back. His cock bobbed heavily. With his left hand, J.J. began to stroke his long shaft.

"Think only of me, Alexa. I'm going to fuck you, gently at first, and then when I take your virginity, you'll feel me inside you, pushing deep. I'm going to push so deep inside you, you'll never forget me..."

His hand moved on his penis as his other fingers played with her, making her squirm and nearly scream.

"Fucking you hard until you can't feel anything but me, and you're getting so damn hot as my cock takes you hard and fast because it wants inside your sweet pussy, claiming every single, silky, wet inch of you."

A low moan escaped her as she saw the image he verbally painted. J.J.'s naked, muscular body straddling hers, his enormous shaft straining in eagerness as it nudged inside her.

Her core clenched. Alexa tossed her head, the cascade of feelings tumbling through her with frightening speed. Desire. A rill of fear. And sheer need.

The long, slow strokes on his cock ceased. The thick head of his engorged penis was purple and more moisture seeped from the slit.

He moved his finger inside her wet core and circled her clit with his thumb.

"I'm readying you now, *cariño*. Feel me now inside you, doesn't that feel good, you're so wet and your honey is drenching me, ah, shit, your scent is driving me out of my fucking mind."

He slid his finger upward, hitting a sensitive spot and she shrieked. The rubbing continued, growing faster and faster as the erotic pleasure increased. The coiled tension in her loins built higher and higher until every inch of her body strained. Strained to touch him, to feel his warm flesh beneath her trembling fingers, to guide his thick shaft inside her.

"That's it, my sweet girl, let go, let go, come for me," he commanded.

Then his finger hit that spot again, as his thumb circled, and she arched upward with a loud shriek of his name. The tension shattered.

Her body shook with hard violence, the shudders frightening and yet so real, her sobs of pleasure turned into gurgling laughter.

Alexa fell back to the mattress, her breath heaving in and out of lungs. Emotions rolled through her like water, filling the empty places. Overwhelmed with joy and pleasure, she gulped down air. He had done this, this werewolf who had seduced her. Emotion filled his own gaze as he quietly watched her.

Hooking his hands through her long hair, he kissed her deeply then pulled back on his haunches. She caught sight of the massive, hard phallus ready to invade her and shivered.

Her heart turned over. Here was a wolf who could tear apart his enemies with his bare hands, and yet he'd delivered nothing but pleasure. She drew in breath sharp with need as he drew her close and nuzzled the sensitive skin of her neck. J.J. nipped gently, then licked the spot. Warm breath feathered over her ear as he whispered.

"I'll make it good for you. Will you let me, Alexa? Will you trust me on this?"

He drew back and she saw the fierce desire in his blue eyes. This was what she'd dreamed for her first time. Alexa wrapped her arms around him and dragged him down for a long, drugging kiss. Then he broke away, mounted her with his strong, hard body.

J.J. lifted himself up on his elbows and guided his penis to her wet, swollen entrance. Sexual excitement raced through her, darkened by a natural fear. She was about to give her untried body to this strong male. But the wolf inside her urged her to relax, prodded by the primitive desire to mate.

He kissed her again and nibbled along her lower lip, coaxing out another wave of pleasure. Then he pushed forward a little and she felt the thickness between her legs start to breach the part of her no male had ever touched.

"Look at me, Alexa," he commanded.

Alexa tensed and clutched his muscular shoulders for support as he began to push inside. He felt impossibly thick, unrelenting, as he penetrated, stretching her wider with each gentle thrust.

It hurt badly. She gritted her teeth and then he gave a sudden, powerful thrust forward, breaching the barrier of her innocence. Stifling a cry, she felt impaled as her wet, sensitive tissues tried to adjust to the demanding invasion.

"Easy," he crooned. "Relax. I know it hurts but trust me, it will get better."

Sinew and muscles bunched and coiled in his arms as he moved over her. Alexa clutched his arms as he slid over her, the springy hairs on his chest teasing against her sensitive breasts.

Instinct took over and she snaked her arms around his neck, urging him onward. He began to move inside her, slowly pulling out, and then pushing forward. Alexa wrapped her legs around his pumping hips, urging him closer. She dug her fingers into his shoulders, the pain lessening, replaced with the incredible sensation of being one with him, this hardened cowboy who'd shown her such passion.

Going still, J.J. gazed down at her, his expression intent. A bead of sweat rolled off his forehead, splashed onto her breast. "Look at me, my darling Alexa."

She stared up into his fierce gaze, and pumped her hips upward. He began thrusting harder. Beneath them, the mattress squeaked as his thrusts became harder, more demanding and then he flung his head back. His powerful body convulsed and bucked as he cried out her name, the hot gush of his seed filling her.

Sweat dampened his dark hair, beaded on his temple. Panting, he looked at her. He murmured something, touching her cheek in a tender gesture, then gently separated their bodies.

Alexa felt dazed and yet a part of her remained sharp and aware.

It was over, and she was no longer a virgin.

And she had a hell of lot of questions for this wolf to answer...

CHAPTER 10

J.J.'s heart hammered against his chest. Sensual awareness filled him as he rolled off Alexa and gathered her into his arms. Never was he more fully aware of his body, the sweat pooling beneath him on the sheets, the tension in his muscles gradually fading, the delicious after effects of dazed bliss humming through his body.

Never had he felt more fully alive, or aware.

Mine.

She was his. He had seduced her with pleasure, branded himself upon her body, taken her innocence. No other male would touch her but him. He didn't give a damn what it took, he would have her as his mate.

He laid a flat palm on the slight roundness of her belly, then stroked her soft skin, imagining it would be like this always. Waking up in bed next to his Alexa, making love.

Making babies.

She would be so beautiful carrying his children. J.J. thought of her belly growing rounded with his child and hunger stirred him all over.

Bracing himself on one elbow, he slid his other palm

up her trembling body. He gently cupped a breast, teasing the nipple with a flick of his thumb. It grew hard and taut beneath his attention.

He looked at her face, the sleepiness in her beautiful eyes, her pink mouth swollen from his possessive kisses.

How he yearned for her, her scent filling his nostrils. He leaned over her and kissed her trembling abdomen, feeling her skin warm beneath his mouth.

He wanted to fuck her from behind, the plump halves of her heart-shaped ass cushioning his hips as he drove hard and fast into her. Fuck her like the wolf he was.

Alexa rubbed her palm across his chest. Desire filled him, his cock stirring anew at her gentle touch. He could make love to her for hours and still want her all over again.

"What did you mean, you don't care about Jeremiah Taylor anymore? He's your alpha."

J.J. tunneled his fingers through her long, silky hair. Gods he had dreamed of this, Alexa in his arms, her long hair spread over his pillow. *Mine.*

"I am Jeremiah Jackson Taylor." He blew a soft breath against her neck. "Don't you know by now?"

She went still. "The billionaire? But you said you were J.J…"

"J.J. around the ranch. The cowboy who makes sure everything gets done. My alter ego, the man who does business, who bought your virginity to free you from Daniel's pack, is Taylor."

"Not Raphael…"

"Raphael is my friend. He came here to help me establish the ranch and act as my beta."

152

And then he looked into her eyes again. They were not clouded with passion, but sharp with anger.

Oh shit.

Alexa slid away from his touch and sat up, clutching the sheet to her breasts. "Gods damn you, J.J.!"

Shaking off the lassitude of erotic bliss, Alexa let her anger rise. Her wolf had refused to entertain thought, driven by the primal need to mate. Her wolf's need for sensual pleasure had been sated.

Now the woman surfaced, the woman who felt betrayed, confused and furious.

"You deliberately led me on, made me think Raphael was Taylor? Are you Taylor? Or is this another game, seducing me before Taylor can claim what is his?"

He watched her quietly. The wolf had taken her and shown her immense sensual pleasure. But she wanted answers. Now.

"Who are you? The truth, this time. There is no Jeremiah Jackson Taylor is there?"

"Yes, there is. I am Jeremiah Jackson Taylor." He calmly met her stunned gaze, his expression slightly arrogant. There was the alpha she'd seen lurking beneath the façade of the insouciant cowboy. "J.J. Owner of the Double B Ranch, the billionaire who bought your virginity."

Alexa's mouth closed. Heat suffused her face as her fingers tightened on the sheets. "You lied to me, you bastard."

"I omitted the truth. I had to, because I couldn't trust you."

153

"You betrayed me. You betrayed my trust." Her voice broke. "Why did you lie? Why couldn't you tell me who you really were?"

His mouth tightened. "I wanted you to know me as who I really am, not the alpha of the most powerful pack in southern Colorado. And I didn't trust that you were not aligned with Daniel. I needed to be sure Daniel did not find out my real identity."

"Working with Daniel? Dear goddess, why the hell would I work with him?!"

"As a businessman, I've interacted with many people over the years, Alexa. I have been betrayed by some, and trust does not come easily to me."

"Me either! You said you wanted a real relationship that was emotional and intimate. But you lied to me. How can you even hope to have a real relationship based on a lie?"

"And you based your feelings on Jeremiah Taylor on gossip and conjecture. You prejudged me because I bought your virginity and you thought I was cold and callous for doing so. Let's talk honestly. You refused to give me a chance."

He drew in a deep breath.

"But it felt good to be myself with you, to shed all that formality and feel comfortable, not having to play the part of the alpha wolf. And then we clicked, really came together. I wanted to tell you the truth, but by then you had offered your virginity for sale. I fell in love with you and would not allow another male to touch you."

Love? He talked of love, but what about trust? Alexa's head swam. Her body felt sore and wonderfully used, but her heart, oh it ached.

"If you're Jeremiah Taylor, then why does the Lupine business database have Raphael's photo as the registered owner and agent authorized to conduct business?"

"Raphael is the agent authorized to conduct business, but not the alpha. If you'd looked further, you'd have seen that it's required only to register the photo of the business agent, not the alpha of each pack. This is to protect certain packs."

He seemed so calm and confident, his blue gaze shuttered.

"Secrets upon secrets. That's what your whole life is."

"Secrets I planned to share with you once you became my mate."

"Your mate? Is that what it's all about? Mates love each other. Jeremiah Jackson Taylor doesn't love. He acquires. That's what you did to me!"

"I gave you what you needed, Alexa. And I want more. I will have more."

Here was the ruthless alpha she'd read about in magazines, the brutal alpha who plowed through others' feelings and didn't give a damn about them.

Alexa scrambled back on her haunches. Her body yearned to draw close, feel more of that delicious erotic pleasure he'd given her, but her mind took control.

"You're a cold-hearted bastard."

"You're right about one thing," he said slowly. "Jeremiah Jackson Taylor is a bastard. A cold, hard-hearted bastard who never hesitates to go after what he wants. He will fight dirty for what he believes in. And I will fight for you, *cariño*. I will fight hard and not fight fair. I will do whatever it takes to win you, and I will be ruthless until you are mine."

155

Clenching her fists, she felt her wolf snarl to the surface, demand to be released. Part sexual, part feral rage, she did not know what ruled her. It didn't matter anymore. Alexa stretched out her fingers, feeling her claws emerge.

She, who prided herself on controlling her wolf, could no longer control the beast. "I don't fight fair, either."

Alexa shifted into her wolf and pounced. The move caught him by surprise. J.J. fell back onto the mattress, his hands flung forward to protect his throat. Her wolf smelled blood on the sheets. Her blood. Semen. His seed. The tangy musk of sex, and J.J.'s delicious spicy scent, all male, triggering her female instinct to mate.

Her wolf raked a claw down his side, demanding he move. J.J. snarled back, his teeth emerging into sharp fangs. With a loud growl, he shifted into his beast and tangled with her, rolling on the mattress, trying to nudge her into the position for mounting. But she was not submissive now, no, too much fury and grief collided within her. Alexa wriggled from beneath him and leapt upon his back, her sharp teeth sinking briefly into the back of his neck.

J.J. snarled and escaped her clutches. In an instant, he mounted her, but he did not bite, did not rake his claws over her thick fur. He merely lay upon her. Not moving, not growling, but letting her feel his muscled body pinning her down with the force of his will.

He was far superior in strength. His massive jaws could snap her neck in half. Alexa recognized this and went still.

Then he did the most extraordinary thing.

J.J. pushed his nose close and licked her muzzle and

whined. It was the call of a male needing his mate. Her wolf recognized the call and her human half wrestled with the mindless fury still claiming her, while her Lupine half urged her to answer him.

Alexa did neither. Instead, she wriggled from beneath him. He offered no resistance. Then she shifted back to her Skin form, watching him with wary eyes.

J.J. shifted back to Skin. Lying on his back, he flung an arm across his forehead, staring at the ceiling.

"I'm sorry for deceiving you, Alexa."

A little mollified, she waited.

"I've spent my life caring only for my desire to make something of myself. For the first time, I realize I must set aside what I want, in order to give you what you need. I love you, Alexa, and I'm willing to prove I'm worthy of your love, of becoming your mate forever."

Her stomach clenched tight. Too much had happened too fast. She didn't know what to think, or if she could trust J.J.

Or Jeremiah, the billionaire, who'd bought her for the night like he bought stocks and bonds.

She'd fallen in love with J.J., but now he'd turned out to be someone else—a Lupine who could buy whatever he wanted, or whomever. A powerful alpha who could dictate her fate.

"How can you prove your love, J.J, when I can't even trust who you are?"

He turned and gathered her hands into his calloused ones. Alexa felt the strength in him, strength of an alpha male who had chosen to work hard alongside his pack. He wasn't at all like Daniel, who lazed about the lodge and denied his pack small privileges.

"Haven't I proven myself all this week through my actions? That's the real me, *cariño*. Jeremiah is my business persona, the male who is ruthless when it comes to money. When it comes to you, I'm equally ruthless. I will never let anyone harm you, let anyone mock you, or try to run your life. If you become my mate, I'll stick by your side and protect you with my blood and bones. And protect your family as well."

Words. Sweet words of devotion. Alexa shook her head. "I want to believe you. But how can I?"

J.J. drew in a deep breath and dropped her hands. "Tomorrow, when Daniel comes here to bring you back to his pack, I'll prove it."

"Right." Alexa scrambled out of bed, suddenly chilled. She reached for the Chinese silk robe and wrapped it around herself. "Prove it, but in the meantime, I've fulfilled my obligation. You got what you paid for, Jeremiah. Now leave me the hell alone."

"Alexa..."

"I'm sleeping by myself. I don't owe you anything anymore."

She didn't turn around as she walked out the door, slamming it behind her. As she ran back to the guest house, tears rose to her eyes. Alexa let them trickle down her cheeks.

No one could see her, anyway.

CHAPTER 11

Monday morning, she had no appetite for breakfast.

After showering and going downstairs, she made coffee and took it onto the back porch.

As she sat, staring at the distant mountains, footsteps sounded. Alexa glanced up as Jane joined her. The crystal dangled from her fingers.

"You forgot this. Found it on the sofa."

A flush tinted Alexa's cheeks. "You can keep it."

"It's meant to protect you."

So Jane knew everything as well. "I'm my own best protection. Tell me, where is he?" Alexa asked, sipping her coffee.

"Who? J.J. or Jeremiah?"

"Does it matter?"

Jane nodded. "They're not the same, you know. J.J. is all we ever see around here. All we ever call him. Only Raphael has to deal with Jeremiah and the business side of the pack. When Jeremiah's side, the business side, comes out, J.J. turns pretty ruthless. It's how he keeps us fed and warm through the winter."

"He should have told me."

"And what would you have done? Turned around

159

and left? Not given him a chance?" The older Lupine shook her head. "He's the best damn thing that ever happened to this pack and that male deserves to be loved. If you're smart, and I believe you are, you'll set aside your stubborn pride and admit how you feel about him."

"I have no stubborn pride!"

Jane gave a sage smile and put the crystal in the pocket of her blue housedress. "Yes, you do. How else could you have cared for your family all these years? J.J. called us all together this morning and told us everything. We're behind you 100 percent, Alexa, if you would do us the honor of becoming our female alpha."

"I don't even know if I can leave Daniel's pack. I don't trust him."

Jane patted her hand. "Don't worry. I trust my alpha, and that's all both of us need. He'll find a way. He always does."

Reality pulled up in a taxi that afternoon. She watched from the guest house as Daniel climbed out. She didn't know where J.J. was, but did it matter? She must confront Daniel first, and demand her freedom.

His belly oozing over a leather belt, he climbed the steps of the main house and sat on a wicker chair on the porch, propping a shoe on the cocktail table. The Lupine's casual rudeness angered her. Alexa reached the porch steps and stood there, arms folded.

"You need to announce yourself. This isn't your ranch, so get your damn feet off the table."

His beady eyes turned hard. "You ordering me about, Alexa? Seven days away from the pack and you've turned into a spoiled princess?"

"Do as she says. She's the authority on this ranch. Get off the porch," a stern female voice ordered.

Jane stood at the front door. She looked like she could sumo wrestle Daniel and win.

With a nod to Jane, Alexa walked over to the enormous oak tree by the house. The tree had guarded the land for years, J.J. had told her. It had become infested with disease two years ago, but he'd worked hard to treat the disease, consulting with arborists and spending money.

Daniel would not take such care, nor patience. He would simply chop it down.

With a sulky look, Daniel joined her, jamming his hands into his trouser pockets. "You've gotten awfully cocky, Alexa, but it ends now. The money was wired to my account this morning. I've come to escort you back home."

"I'm not going. Not yet. Not until you hear what I have to say."

"Are you deaf, Alexa? Get your bags and let's go."

"Why are you so eager to get me back? You hate me. I hate you."

"I changed my mind. You will honor the blood oath."

She sensed another reason.

"You have your money. I want my family released from the blood oath now. I've fulfilled the terms of the contract."

He looked sly. "I should get you back as quickly as possible, for your father's sake."

161

Her heart sank to her stomach. "What's wrong with him?"

"He fell off the back steps."

Bile and panic rose in her throat. Oh gods, she'd been afraid of something bad happening to her father. "When? Is he okay?"

Daniel studied his grimy fingernails. "Maybe. It happened a few days ago. You won't want to leave your poor papa. He's far too weak to be moved from the lodge."

Alexa felt all her hopes shatter into thousands of shards. But she'd anticipated this move and she wasn't as helpless as he thought. "You bastard. You never told me he'd fallen."

"I didn't want to interrupt your vacation."

"Vacation! You wanted me to go through with this to humiliate me, and you never intended to let me go." A horrifying suspicion filled her. "He was steady on his feet when I last saw him. You pushed him!"

Daniel chuckled. "Now, Alexa, all I did was offer a friendly pat on the back. Was it my fault that he couldn't stand straight?"

Rage filled her. She wanted to kick and pummel him, but one thing she had learned from the ancient Lupine texts was that if she did, Daniel would be within his rights to kill her.

Her family needed her now more than ever.

The front door opened and J.J. stepped outside. He left the porch and approached them, looking over Daniel with a tight-lipped expression. Daniel stared at him.

Thumbs hooked into his belt, J.J. wore a tanned Stetson, faded jeans and a blue chambray shirt. He looked every inch the cowboy, and nothing like a powerful billionaire.

Daniel stood a foot shorter than J.J. and his belly oozed over his belt buckle like gelatin. As they stood side by side, Alexa noticed the stark contrast. With his easy grace and muscled body, J.J. was strikingly handsome.

Daniel was an overweight sour wolf.

Sliding an arm around her waist, J.J. faced Daniel. "You can't have Alexa back. I'm formally claiming her."

Daniel shook his head. "She's mine. From my pack."

"You will not have her, Daniel. She's mine, and will stay mine. Her family will be under my protection as well."

Alexa looked at J.J. in sheer misery. "I have to return with him. My father is injured. I have no choice. I'll never be free."

"Name your price for freeing Alexa from your pack," J.J. told Daniel.

"There is no price. You can't have her, cousin." Daniel's mouth lifted in an ugly sneer. "Cousin?" Alexa blinked. How many more shocks could she endure in one day?

"On my father's side," J.J. said in rapid Spanish.

"Speak English," Daniel demanded.

J.J. spoke slowly. "If you won't release Alexa and her family, then you leave me no choice. I'm coming with her."

"What?" Daniel stepped back and looked dumbfounded, and a little afraid. It was as if no one had ever dared to stand up to him. The idea fed her strength.

J.J. turned to Alexa. "I'm sticking to your side like super glue and if Daniel won't release you, then I'll go with you."

Stunned, she stared at him, her heart turning over. Not daring to believe the words he'd said. "You'd give up everything here… for me?"

J.J. turned and the look in his eyes took her breath away. "A-always did s-s." He dragged in a deep breath and said in Spanish. "I always promised myself when I met the right female to become my mate, the most important thing in my life would be her. But I refuse to go as your friend."

He slid to his knees, took her hand. "Alexa, I can't wait to formally mate you. Will you be mine?"

Tears burned her eyes. For once, she let them fall. "Yes."

"You can't do that. You need my permission to mate, Alexa." Daniel laughed. "And the only way I'd let this bastard mate you and enter my pack is if he gives me all his money. All of it! He's too damn greedy. He'll never do it."

J.J. took a deep breath. "Fine. If that is what it takes, you can have my wealth."

She ignored Daniel's outraged shout as J.J. rose off his knees and kissed her, his mouth warm and firm against hers. He'd made up his mind. Determined to fight for her, he'd give up everything for Alexa. The ranch. His position as alpha. Even his life as Jeremiah Jackson Taylor.

"I love you, *cariño*. I told you, I will have you as my mate. If you'll have me for life, I'm not letting anyone stand in my way. I'll give up all my money to Daniel and join you in his pack. At least there I can be with you." His mouth compressed in that stubborn line she'd come to know well.

"I want to mate you because you make me happy. Because I make you happy, because we're good together and I need you at my side, ruling my pack, making it strong. I need you, Alexa. I need your strength, your humor, your compass-sion..."

He clasped her hands and looked her in the eyes, his gaze darkening. "I need you because I love you."

A thick lump clogged her throat. No one, not even her family, had every sacrificed so much for her. And J.J. was giving up everything, all his wealth and power, to humble himself by joining his nasty cousin's pack, just so they could be together.

When he pulled away, he gathered her into his arms, his chin resting atop her head. She could feel the tension knit his muscles.

"Oh this is sickening! So sweet I want to vomit. Having you in my pack, cuz? And all your money? It might be worth it to have you there as Alexa's mate. I'll make you regret every single moment you're under my control." Daniel laughed and it was an ugly sound, like steel scraping against slate.

Alexa looked deep into J.J.'s eyes. "I love you. You'd do all that for me?"

"Tell her in English, J.J."

J.J.'s mouth worked violently.

"Tell her! Oh wait, you can't. Because you can't speak without making a damn fool of yourself. F-f-fool."

"Alexa," J.J. whispered.

"Tell her how you feel, in English and maybe I'll let you mate with her. It's within my right to keep Alexa tied to my pack. She signed an agreement." Daniel narrowed his eyes. "Tell her how much you love her, just like you told Selena all those years ago. Tell her about Selena. How she loved you soooo much. Fool."

A haunting pain shadowed J.J.'s eyes. He pulled away from her, his mouth opening and closing as if he were struggling to breathe. Alexa's stomach twisted and she had a sickening suspicion.

"It's okay, J.J. You don't have to tell me."

He spoke in rapid Spanish. "Yes, I do. After last night, Alexa, I swore to never keep secrets from you again."

"J.J., she started.

Torment filled his blue eyes. "Selena was gorgeous, a female who joined the pack when I turned 15. At first, she only seemed to be interested in Daniel. And then one day she asked to walk with me in the woods. For three weeks, she met me after school and we'd make out. And then one day she told me she wanted us to be lovers and told me to meet her at the barn that night."

"Oh no," Alexa said softly in Spanish. "I think I know what you're going to say."

"I went into the barn. Selena was standing in the shadows. She said she wanted me to be her first lover. It was fucking freezing and I told her we could go to my room, but she worried about us being caught. She asked me to strip naked."

J.J. drew in a deep breath. "I did. Standing there, shivering in the barn, in the dark, I scented her, heard her draw near… That's when the lights came on."

Squeezing his fists, he slowed his speech, his Spanish nearly slurring. Gods, she wanted to retch at the glee on Daniel's face, the triumph.

"You were set up," she said, sickened.

"Daniel stood there, surrounded by all the other females in the pack around our age. He roared with laughter, and pointed at my dick. All the females, including Selena, laughed at me and jeered. Then Daniel kissed Selena. All I could do was stammer like a fool, 'Y-you l-l-ove m-e. Y-ou s-said so.' And they all laughed and called me a stuttering loser."

Daniel laughed. "You are a loser, J.J. Enough Spanish. Tell her you love her in English, fool. Tell her and I'll let her and her family go."

J.J. closed his eyes and opened them. Her lover spread his arms open wide, as if exposing himself as an open target.

"A-a-lexa, I l-l-ove y-you. I, I a-always h-h-have, f-rom the m-moment I s-saw y-ou."

"I l-l-ove y-y-ou." Daniel sneered at him. "How can you stand this stuttering fool, Alexa? He can't even talk! Never could! That's why he speaks to you in Spanish. He hasn't spoken to a woman in English without stuttering since we were young. Do you really want this loser?"

She stared at J.J., not seeing Daniel, barely hearing him, and suddenly everything made sense. Why he wanted to disguise himself, why he distanced himself from women and why he reverted to another language. And this brave Lupine had the courage to expose his flaws in front of her. His pain. His vulnerability.

"He is not a loser," she said loudly. "Leave him alone, you sick freak. He's worth ten thousand of you."

Damnit, J.J. deserved happiness, and he was standing here, right before her, baring his soul. Her heart turned over.

"I love you too, J.J. Jeremiah. I don't care who you are or how you say it." She cupped his cheek and let all her feelings show. "A rich businessman or a poor cowboy, I love you."

J.J. closed his eyes and pulled her into his arms. She hugged him tight, feeling the entire world could collapse but it didn't matter, as long as they had each other.

She turned around and faced Daniel, confidence filling her. Now she had the best reason of all for leaving. "You're a fool. I don't care what kind of contract my family signed with you. You can't hold us in your pack forever. I love J.J. and I will find a way to be free of you, and take my family with me."

"You're the fool, Alexa. He's not going to live long enough for you to have sex with him again. I'll have you first, bitch mouth."

And then Daniel stepped back, his face bulging, his belly expanding until he looked pregnant, his eyes growing to two dots in a doughy face. Buttons popped like champagne corks as his torso grew. The neatly pressed designer trousers split and then fell to the ground.

What stood before them was a pale-skinned mass of doughy flesh with two bright eyes, a slit of a nose and a red slash for a mouth. No penis. No thatch of pubic hair. No gender at all. Panic rose in her throat and her wolf whined, wanting to run in terror from this thing.

Dimly she thought this was why Daniel never liked women. Or men. And then she remembered the flash of kindness Daniel had shown long ago. He was two different people.

"Live long enough," it gurgled. Then it opened the

slit of a mouth, showing rows of sharp, shiny teeth, pointed as a shark's. "I'll tear you apart."

"Oh dear gods," she rasped, wanting to gag on the nausea and terror rising in her throat. "What are you?"

J.J. shoved her behind him and growled deep. "Go back to the house, Alexa."

She wildly searched for a weapon, but found nothing in the yard. Hell, could she even kill this thing, whatever it was? It looked ready to divide in half, split into thousands of gelatinous Daniel-things, smothering them to death...

We're going to get killed by the Pillsbury Dough Boy. Oh dear gods, this can't be happening...

"What is it?" she shrieked.

"Changeling Gnome. Rafe's tangled with a few in his past." J.J. balled his fists and growled deep in his throat. "You will not have her. She's mine. Get it?"

Mouth yawning open, he growled, showing long white fangs glistening in the sunlight. Alexa stepped back, searching the yard again for a weapon, for anything that would thwart the Gnome.

As J.J. leapt into the air, starting to shift into wolf, Alexa saw a flash of silver and screamed. "He's got a knife!"

The thing slashed and then stabbed J.J. as the Lupine leapt through the air, the angry snarl turning into a howl of pain. Naked, J.J. fell back to the earth in Skin form, his face contorted, his mouth gasping. Blood seeped from his belly around the knife handle protruding from it.

"Half-breed," the thing chortled. "Half-breed! I killed your old man, I'll kill you! He never committed suicide. I did it, I did it, I watched him spin in the wind."

Alexa growled and shifted into her wolf. Racing forward, she leapt at Daniel, aiming for his groin. Hell, there had to be a groin. *Doesn't this gnome-thing have balls?*

As she head-butted him, she met pure buoyant flesh and was repelled, like a child in a bounce house. Dazed, she shook her head, growled and rushed forward again.

The Daniel-thing threw a web of sticky, gooey flesh at her. It touched her fur and forced her to shift back to Skin, the web turning into a sticky spider's web. Frantic, she struggled to release herself from the crisscross of silk, feeling tiny legs scamper toward her mouth…

From the direction of the barn, several cowboys raced forward, led by Raphael. Waving a hand, the Daniel-thing released a blob of pale doughy flesh. It sailed through the air and landed on them, smothering them in a net similar to the one encasing Alexa. Raphael freed himself and raced forward, but a large rock sailed through the air and slammed him on the forehead.

He went down hard and lay still.

The whisper of tiny spiders crawled over her bare flesh. Naked, she struggled against the web-net imprisoning her, swallowing her gorge. Spiders, oh gods, she hated these.

Then she saw J.J., blood streaming from his torso. Alexa brushed the spiders off and called upon her wolf's courage. Screw the spiders. She had to save J.J.

Now that she'd finally found someone who loved her, there was no way in hell she was letting him die.

White-hot pain burned J.J.'s stomach. He struggled to breathe and tamp down panic as adrenalin flooded his system. He was strong, but losing blood.

Daniel spoke through a grossly misshapen mouth. "You thought yourself better than me, better than me because you were taller and stronger. But I have the power. I made sure of it that day I went into the forest and found my true self, as I am now. Power, more magick than you could ever hope for. I was the one who put the leeches in your bed and locked Alexa in the shed with the spiders. I did all those things and you never knew. I've been hiding here all along. Recognize this?"

His cousin vanished. In his place was a small, cheerful gnome with a bright red cap. The same one Alexa had brought with her from home.

Daniel rematerialized. "So easy to mimic that gnome. I have powers you can only imagine!"

Then he waved a hand and a rope with a noose dangled from the thick limb of the oak tree. Daniel jerked the noose tight around J.J.'s neck and pulled the rope hard. He managed to get a hand between his throat and the noose before Daniel pulled him into the air. Gasping, J.J. struggled for oxygen, his right hand fighting to loosen the rope about his neck, his left hand fumbling to pull free the blade buried in his stomach.

"Let's swing, cuz! Remember how you liked to swing on the tire?" Daniel screamed.

He pushed J.J. forward. Searing pain burned his stomach from the knife.

He had to kill this bastard, kill him before he destroyed Alexa. Gasping, he pulled the knife free, biting back a scream from the pain, feeling warm blood spill over his hand. J.J. reached up and sawed at the rope, struggled to be free of the noose.

He needed air now, or he was going to strangle to death, hearing that maniacal laugher in his death throes...

The rope snapped and he spilled to the ground. Still clutching the knife, J.J. staggered to his feet, feeling grayness push around the edges of his consciousness. He watched the knife fall to the ground, felt blood gush through his fingers.

Alexa. He must kill Daniel to save Alexa. If he died today, he would die with her name on his lips, trying to keep her safe. His mate. His love.

Alexa. He turned and saw his love, his life, fight the massive spider's web encasing her, ignoring the small black spiders crawling over her bare skin. Alexa hated spiders, feared them, but she fought as if they weren't there.

He spied the cord of wood by the steps. Wood. Fire. *Fire.* Rafe always left the lighter by the wood, he did it for the fire pit so they could sit around and have a beer or a whiskey on those bitterly cold winter nights...

With his last ounce of strength, J.J. staggered over to the wood pile, pain from the knife blade eating into his internal organs, burning him with agony. *Save Alexa, save her, you can do it...*

His thumb flicked the lighter's wheel. Failed. J.J. groaned and used both hands to flick the lighter, blood streaming down his belly to his groin, staining the earth.

Got it. He picked up a piece of wood and prayed. *Please light, please light...*

"Are you dead yet?" Daniel giggled, the sound like razors slicing across slate.

The delicate blue flame caught, flickered like faint hope. And then it grew stronger and brighter even as J.J.'s vision grew dimmer.

Wait for it. Have patience, Raphael said. Patience. I have none. Have to make my millions, billions, prove I'm someone, prove I'm the best.... but I'm nothing without my Alexa...

He smelled the humid, wet scent of Daniel, like moldy bread, and turned, the wood clutched in his hands like a sword.

He thrust it at his cousin, straight into his fat, fleshy belly. Daniel staggered back and screamed, the fire licking his pale flesh, eating his doughy skin that was not Skin.

J.J. fell to the ground.

He watched Daniel burn, the flames cheerfully consuming the strange dough-man as if the yard was a giant oven, his cousin not screaming now, but quiet, until there remained nothing but a blackened husk.

Then the web holding Alexa prisoner vanished. She rushed forward as J.J. collapsed on the ground.

Her warm arms surrounded him. He struggled to breathe. Gods, his stomach and throat hurt like a bitch. He was dying, but Alexa was safe. All that mattered.

"Please, J.J., don't die on me," she sobbed.

Brave Alexa, his Alexa, who never cried in front of others, now crying, her warm salty tears raining on his face. Too late.

And then as his vision began to wink out, he saw the blackened husk of Daniel sit up.

It wasn't over.

CHAPTER 12

Daniel wasn't dead.

Fury coiled her muscles, turned her into a raging wolf. Alexa very gently laid J.J. back on the ground and shifted into wolf.

Snarling, she raced forward, bit into the blackened thing that was Daniel. She tore at his flesh, but even as she did, the burnt skin turned pink and healed.

Daniel laughed and swatted at her, sending her sailing backward. Alexa slammed into the porch, feeling as if she'd been hit by a steel beam.

"Alexa!" J.J. screamed. He staggered to his feet, picked up the smoldering wood.

Her lover, her life, somehow got to Daniel and hit him hard. He kept smashing his body. There was no blood, only pieces of pale flesh splattering on the ground like harmless bits of dough.

Daniel finally lay still. Then his body jerked.

"He's still alive?" Alexa cried out. "Dear goddess, how do you kill this thing?"

Suddenly a brilliant silver light appeared in a flash of pure energy. A handsome man dressed in black stood before her. The man's hair was ebony, each strand tipped with silver.

Tristan, the Silver Wizard, guardian of all shifters and one of the four members of the Brehon, the wizards who ruled over Others.

Alexa shifted back to Skin and clothed herself by magick.

The wizard touched J.J. and the bloodied wound on his belly vanished. Tristan stepped back, watching both of them with a speculative look.

"I didn't call for you," J.J. rasped.

Tristan flicked a finger at Raphael, who walked toward them. His beta rubbed at a terrible head wound and examined his reddened fingers with a rueful look. "I called him. I figured you needed help, J.J. Those Changeling Gnomes don't fuck around."

"How could you tell what Daniel was?" Alexa asked. "I've lived with him and he always seemed different, but I never suspected he wasn't Lupine."

"I tangled with them. They have a faint stench when their true essence comes through. It smells like rotting fish." Raphael wiped his bloodied fingers against his blue chambray shirt.

"Or human body odor or something else as repulsive, depending upon what an Other finds most disgusting. The Brehon cursed them with this stench as a protective measure, should an Other tangle with them." The Silver Wizard touched Raphael's head and the wound immediately healed.

"Thanks." Raphael nodded and then looked down at Daniel's prone form. "I'll assure the others the threat is gone. They were pretty shaken when they couldn't help protect you both."

He gave Alexa a solemn look. "Because that is what pack does...we protect the alpha couple with our lives."

As Raphael walked away, Tristan folded his arms and studied Daniel's prone form.

"You're safe now. However, there is the matter of your cousin to deal with. This is not Daniel. Daniel has been possessed by this Changeling Gnome."

"I've known him all my life. How could this happen?" J.J. asked.

Tristan squatted on the ground and drew a rune in the dirt. "The real Daniel is locked inside this body, possessed by the Gnome. Changeling Gnomes take on the characteristics of their hosts, along with their powers. They surrender their natural powers to live in a host's body, but they can still mimic inanimate objects, which is what makes them so damn dangerous. You can't tell if the object is a gnome or something harmless."

The wizard dusted off his hands. "Once Gnomes absorb the blood of a powerful alpha Lupine, their magick increases. They can use telekinesis on inanimate objects through a warding spell. They can even imitate Others, once they touch the Other they wish to imitate. They become harder to kill. They can burn, but reanimate."

"That's why Daniel put the leeches in my bed. He wanted my blood," J.J. realized aloud.

"And Daniel imitated Raphael and you... Daniel locked me in the shed. He also imitated my gnome statue and I carried him here." Alexa felt sick.

The wizard nodded. "It is extremely difficult to discern them from the original host, even for a wizard such as myself. By the time we suspect what it is, the gnome has shifted into another form."

Standing, Tristan directed energy at the bits of flesh Daniel had spilled and they squealed like a living thing before turning into ash.

"Is he dead?" Alexa moved closer to J.J. He put a comforting arm around her shoulders.

"Not yet," Tristan said.

"You can't kill him?" J.J. asked.

"I could try baking him to death. I do fancy muffins with fresh butter. Do you happen to have an industrial oven handy?"

When they simply stared at him, the wizard sighed. "No one has a sense of humor anymore. Yes, I can kill him, but I'll kill whatever remains of your cousin hiding deep inside him. It's a delicate process. Requires an expert. I hate this job sometimes." Tristan looked upward with a resigned expression. "Xavier!"

Nothing.

"He's never around when you need him. Xavier!!!"

"Who is Xavier?" J.J. asked.

"The Crystal Wizard. Ruler of Earthers, such as trolls, ogres or gnomes, all those disgusting creatures. No wonder he hides. His charges are always causing trouble. XAVIER!!!!! I'll have to do this the old fashioned way."

Tristan stood and stretched out his hands to the sky and chanted. A minute later there was an explosion of silver smoke. Out of the cloud rode a man dressed in shining white on a BMX motorbike. With a flourish, the rider ground the crotch rocket to a halt. He shut off the engine and dismounted, removing a white helmet set with sparkling white crystals. He had long brown hair tumbling past his shoulders, each strand tipped with gleaming quartz crystal. His face was pale as alabaster and his eyes glittered like diamonds. J.J. blinked, finding it hard to look at him. He was shiny as pure ice reflected by bright sunlight.

Tristan gave a disgusted snort. "Always the showman."

"You rang?" Xavier drawled. The wizard spoke in tones of the Deep South.

"Where the hell have you been?"

"Partying in Nawlins, having a good time with a frisky young enchantress who was quite limber and loves to ride me while I ride my motorcycle." He patted the bike. "She is quite flexible. Does this marvelous thing with her toes… is there is a good reason you interrupted my vacation?"

"You're always on vacation." Tristan gestured to Daniel, who began to rise again with a snarl. He shot a bolt of energy at Daniel, who collapsed.

"You need to extract the original before he dies from all the energy I've tossed at him."

Xavier's expression hardened. Tossing aside the helmet, he squatted down by Daniel. The wizard ran a hand over his body. "Damnit. I know the Changeling Gnome who took over this body. His name is Thall. I thought I had locked up all of these things."

"Obviously one escaped and possessed Daniel."

"It's a difficult matter. The boy inside could already be dead." He placed a hand on Thall's chest. "Daniel is still inside, but barely. I can get him out." Xavier sighed. "I knew it was going to be a bitch of a day when I woke up and there was no chicory coffee left. Stand back. This is going to get very ugly. Tristan, I'll need a warm blanket, and your help to clean up the...mess."

Tristan flicked his fingers and a thick blanket appeared in his hands. He held it and stood nearby.

J.J. moved back, tucking Alexa's head against his chest to shield her from having to see. He himself watched. Xavier murmured a chant over the Gnome, who snarled and tried to rise. The Crystal Wizard pressed his thumb against the thing's heart. The creature gasped and fell backward, staring sightlessly at the sky.

"He's dead," Xavier said flatly. "I have to act quickly, before the boy inside him dies, too."

Suddenly Xavier turned into a crystalline buzz-saw the size of a dinner plate. The saw whirled through the air as Tristan stood nearby, the breeze created by the saw billowing Tristan's long black hair.

Xavier sliced through the body from crotch to neck. The skin split open like a zipper opening on a body bag. There was no blood, no ooze of entrails. But a human hand suddenly emerged from the opening Xavier had created. The wizard shifted back, reached inside the body and tugged out a boy of about 12. The boy collapsed on the ground, wet, shivering and naked.

"Dear mother goddess," J.J. breathed. "*Daniel*."

His cousin, the boy he'd played with, climbed trees with, and had been best friends with.

Xavier covered the boy with the thick blanket, lifted him gently from the now shriveling body. Tristan flicked a hand at the corpse, which burst into flame and then turned to ash.

"He will need immediate care. All his memories of growing into adulthood are gone. He will only recall meeting the gnome who absorbed him." Xavier sighed as he set Daniel on the ground. "I'll have to find him an adoptive family willing to raise him, one that will be patient and kind."

Tristan looked at J.J. and Alexa.

J.J.'s chest tightened. "I will take him into my pack. He's blood. I owe him."

Xavier shook his head. "After all he's done to you?"

"It wasn't him. Not his fault." J.J. struggled with his emotions. "Daniel was nothing but kind to me before he changed."

"How boringly noble these Lupines of yours are, Tristan. I do believe I shall gag."

Tristan gave a slow smile. "Don't be envious, X. You don't look good in that shade of green. You'll have to stick around for a while as needed, to make certain all the elements of the dark spell are gone from Daniel."

Xavier nodded, his expression hard. "First I have a little housecleaning to do. When I find the one who released this Gnome from its prison, he will regret tampering with my territory."

The wizard waved a hand. He, the motorbike and helmet vanished in a puff of white smoke.

"Always the theatrics." Tristan shook his head.

"What prison did he put the gnomes into?" Alexa asked. She sat next to Daniel and pulled him into her arms, rocking him back and forth. Daniel rested against her and stopped shivering.

She had such a good heart, J.J. realized. She would make an excellent mother, first to Daniel, who needed plenty of guidance, and later, to their own young.

"The worst," Tristan said solemnly. "A prison of pure crystal, where there is nothing but reflection of themselves, staring at four mirrored walls of shiny crystal until their minds are gone. I have heard the screams. They are quite haunting."

The Silver Wizard cocked his head. "Ah, I believe you're about to have another visitor. I would stick around for the fun, but I'm late for my hair appointment."

Tristan vanished in a puff of silver smoke.

Jane emerged from the main house with her mate, Emmanuel. They took the real Daniel into the house, promising to care for him.

"You okay?" J.J. asked, framing Alexa's face with his hands.

"I'm not the one who had a knife sticking out of me like a Thanksgiving turkey." She unbuttoned his shirt and ran her hand over his taut, unmarked abdomen. "No marks. It's like it never happened."

"The miracle of the Silver Wizard." J.J. lifted his head as a taxi pulled into the driveway. "Ah. A little late, but he's here."

The taxi stopped and the alpha of the Mitchell pack climbed out of the back. Aiden looked tired, his hair rumpled and his eyes bleary.

As the taxi drove away, J.J. strode toward the alpha and shook his hand. "Thanks for coming. I won't be needing those papers after all, but it's good to have them as backup, in case whoever takes over Daniel's pack wants to pull the same stunt on Alexa."

He explained what happened. Aiden glanced around the yard. "I guess I'm a little late for the party. Too bad. I was looking forward to declaring a pack war on that son of a bitch Daniel."

"I don't understand." Alexa looked at Aiden. "What's going on?"

181

Aiden held out a thick envelope. "All you need to free yourself and your family from Daniel's pack. The signatures of ten alpha Lupines willing to vouch for you. Nine are from myself and the other alphas you worked for this past year." His mouth lifted in a slight grin. "The last signature is from Nikita. She said her pack would fight for you. She took a vote and every single pack member is willing to fight to free you, Alexa, just like me. I can't afford a pack war now, but I'm willing to fight for you if I must."

J.J. turned back to her. "I sent my private jet to fly Aiden down here after I researched the book of texts and found a loophole for you."

"If a Lupine signs a blood contract with an alpha to join his pack, he can be freed through a Declaration of Character by ten alpha Lupines," Aiden recited. "It must be a quorum of no less than ten alpha Lupines who vouch for you to the point of declaring a pack war, if necessary."

Tears burned in the back of her throat. "They'd do it for me?"

J.J. pushed back a lock of hair from her face, his gaze tender as he stared down at her. "And me, because I told them I want you as my mate. I told them they could call in any financial favor, at any time, if they'd do this for you."

"You may go broke," Aiden warned, as Alexa took the envelope. "I know Nikita needs money."

J.J. kept staring at Alexa, his hands warm as he slid them up her arms. "I don't care if I have to give up all my wealth. Alexa is worth it."

His kiss was warm and tender. When they pulled apart, Aiden studied them with a rueful look. "All I ask is that you don't have sex in front of me. My libido can't take it right now."

Dust rose in the air as another taxi rattled down the dirt drive. Alexa shook her head. "What is this, a party?"

The taxi parked. Nikita paid the driver and climbed out, pushing back her long, dark blonde hair. The female alpha joined them, her dark blue eyes blazing with anger. She dumped a backpack on the ground.

"Where's the fight? Where is that son of a bitch?" Nikita cracked her knuckles. "I'd love to give Daniel a piece of my mind. And my fists."

Aiden strode toward her, and seized her hands, rubbing his thumbs over them in long strokes. "That fight is over, sweetheart. Calm down."

The female alpha's eyes widened. She pulled her hands away from Aiden. "You killed him?"

After Alexa explained what happened, Nikita shook her head. "All this bad juju around. I swear, I'll need a vacation soon. I came all the way here for nothing?"

Aiden gave her a slow, appreciative and very male glance. "Not nothing. As long as you're here, we can have lunch. And dinner. And then I'll have you for dessert..."

"Forget it, Mitchell. Now that Alexa is safe, and can legally leave her pack, I have to get back to the ranch." Nikita gave Alexa a warm smile. "When I heard you needed a way to escape that creep Daniel, I bought a plane ticket down here."

"I'll refund the cost of the ticket, and give you a little something extra," J.J. promised.

"Thank you." Remembering how Nikita had nearly torn into Daniel back the Mitchell ranch after the alpha had hit her, Alexa hugged Nikita, grateful to have another female friend who cared. "Can you stay for dinner? I hate that you rushed all the way here for nothing."

"Thanks, but I'd rather visit later, when I have more time."

"Please, take my private plane. I'll have Raphael drive both of you to the airport." J.J. called his beta on the cell. "Rafe, get the Esplanade. I need you to take Aiden and Nikita to the jet."

Nikita gave Aiden a rueful look. "Terrific. I have to ride back with you?"

"Unless you want to drive back with me. I'm sure J.J. would loan us a truck." A wicked spark ignited Aiden's gaze. "I could find us a nice, romantic place to park."

"Forget it, Mitchell. I'd rather walk across broken glass on bare feet than spend hours alone with you." But heat entered Nikita's gaze and Alexa could scent the female's sexual interest.

"Liar," he murmured. "The jet will be faster. Best to get you home quicker, so you can finally set a date for the mating challenge."

Raphael pulled up in a gleaming white Cadillac Esplanade truck. The couple walked off to the waiting truck as Alexa snuggled close to J.J.

She traced his taut jaw. They were finally safe, but one nagging question remained.

"J.J., why did you purchase my virginity? Was it because you wanted a novel experience with a virgin Lupine?"

He picked up her hands and kissed them, his gaze burning into hers. "It was always you. I was furious that you had to resort to selling yourself. I couldn't allow another male to purchase your virginity. Let another male touch you, maybe abuse you or give you an experience that would leave you hurt or afraid? I vowed if it took every penny I had, I wouldn't let that happen."

Warmth filled her. From the very beginning, she'd known this Lupine was special, and the one intended for her. "It's really all over? And we can be mated?"

He caressed her cheek. "Soon as possible. I'm not waiting to make you mine for life."

CHAPTER 13

A few weeks later...

The ancient Lupine law of texts had delivered another boon to J.J. A few days after he officially mated Alexa, in front of her happy family, he united his pack to Daniel's former pack. As first cousin, J.J. inherited control of Daniel's pack until Daniel became old enough to rule.

He immediately set about putting Raphael in charge of organizing the pack and appointing a beta to run things. Jane and her mate, Emmanuel, were patiently teaching the young Daniel how to become Lupine again.

Confident that things would run smoothly in his absence, J.J. took Alexa to the Rocky Mountains.

Late in the afternoon, as they hiked beside a lake on a remote trail in the national park, wind rustled the tree branches. In the distance a bird called. A chipmunk rummaged for food as it neared the bench. Sunlight winked off the granite rocks lining the path. No others were around. They were alone in the woods.

This was a place where a wolf could run wild and

free, surrounded by pine trees and birch and aspen, away from the crowds and the careworn life of Skins. Alexa scuffed the toe of her hiking boot against the dirt.

In a small clearing, J.J. removed a blanket from his backpack and spread it on the forest floor. They ate the picnic dinner she'd packed. Then after, he lay on his side, watching her.

"What's wrong? You look so pensive." Smiling, she bit into an apple. "Is it your Jeremiah side coming out?"

"My Jeremiah side will always be there," he admitted. "But around you, I'm just J.J. All this time it's been me all along, wanting you, wanting us to be together. Jeremiah bought your virginity, Alexa, because I couldn't let someone else take it, but what I need is something I can never buy—your heart."

Setting down the apple, Alexa wrapped her arms around his neck and kissed him. She lovingly brushed back a strand of his black hair. "You have it. Always."

She began to undress. "It's a shame to waste all this privacy. I've always wondered what it would be like to make love in the open."

His blue eyes twinkled. "Tonight is a full moon, too."

Alexa sucked in a breath. The wolf's knot, the legend she'd heard about.

"But it's not nightfall yet..." Disappointment filled her.

J.J. glanced at the setting sun. "Moonrise is soon."

He stripped as well. Then he sat, watching her, his erection thick and heavy, but he made no move.

She understood. The next move was up to her.

Alexa snaked an arm around his neck. She kissed him. Hard. Her tongue delved between his lips and

187

stroked the moist cavern of his mouth. With her other hand, she reached down and cupped his sac.

It was not the kiss of an inexperienced virgin, but the kiss of a woman determined to claim her man.

She spread her legs open and he settled between them, and thrust deep. His lovemaking was hard and fast, and she responded instinctively.

When she climaxed again, he joined her, and for a moment, lay heavily atop her, shuddering. Sweat dripped down his forehead, splashing onto her like teardrops. Her limbs felt shaky, their muscles abused.

Her body felt well-loved and languid with pleasure.

As they lay on the blanket in each other's arms, a different longing now pulled at her. Her wolf itched to race up into the pine forest, leap over fallen deadwood and chase prey. For too long she'd been restricted and caged.

As if he could read her mind, J.J. tugged her hand. "Let's pack up, get dressed and keep hiking. We need to get deeper into the woods where we won't run into Skins."

When they were ready, he led her into the pine forest. Some trees had been destroyed by the pine bark beetle, and he skirted around these carefully. "Avoid widow makers. Those are branches that fall from big trees that died."

A couple of miles later, he dumped his pack and unlaced his hiking boots. J.J. removed his socks and then tugged off his jeans.

Alexa couldn't breathe as she stared at him. He was so magnificent, more than six feet of pure, muscled male.

And all hers. Every single inch.

Alexa shed her clothing and stuffed it into her backpack.

His gaze turned hungry as it roved over her, but the stark male admiration in his eyes made her feel beautiful.

Then he brought their backpacks over to a hollowed log and stuffed them inside. He took her hand and pointed to the sky as the sun began to set.

"Moonrise," he said in a husky voice.

He shifted into wolf. Tall and muscled, he looked proud and strong.

She squatted down and ran a caressing hand through his thick fur. J.J. lifted his muzzle and licked her nipple.

"J.J.!" Alexa laughed as he gave her a big wolfish grin.

She shifted and ran through the open field, the wind ruffling her fur as J.J. chased her. Her senses exploded, nearly making her dizzy. The air felt crisper, the scents of pine and nearby small animals sharp. Her ears pricked as she heard the slapping of the water against the shoreline.

J.J. stopped at a tree, nosed around it and then lifted his leg, making his territory.

Alexa leapt atop a small boulder and released a low howl, relishing the freedom previously denied to her. If only it could always be like this. Her wolf urged her to forget the future, and live for the moment.

They ran through the woods, chasing a chipmunk and then a squirrel, and then found a stream threading through the trees.

They drank.

J.J. nosed her over to a nearby rock by the water. Then he mounted her.

The sex was wilder and more freeing than anything they'd ever done.

And then they shifted back into human form as he bent her over the rock and pounded long and hard into her, one arm firmly encasing her waist, his other hand fisting her long hair.

"Come for me, sweetheart," he growled. "Come on, Alexa."

"J.J.," she cried out.

"Say it, say my name. *Jeremiah,*" he growled, pounding harder into her.

Alexa squeezed her thighs tighter, holding him closer. "Please," she sobbed. "Jeremiah, please, oh gods, let me come!"

And then he gave a slight twist and she shattered, everything rushing together like fireworks, her blood pulsing through her veins, her senses exploding.

A deep growl rumbled from J.J.'s throat. She felt his engorged penis swell, pressing hard against her wet, sensitive tissues. His wolf's knot.

As the protrusion thickened, it rubbed enticingly against nerve endings enriched with blood, filling her with renewed pleasure. J.J. gave one last thrust. Orgasm seized her again, making her shriek, the sound echoing through the forest. Rearing back, J.J. seized her hips and released a long, low howl as a thick stream of semen sprayed hotly against her womb.

For a few minutes, his big body shuddered as he continued to climax, each jettison of hot seed sending her into another orgasm. Finally his climax slowed.

Then he collapsed atop her, the sweat of their bodies mingling.

He rolled off her as his wolf's knot shrank, and then

carefully pulled out. Then he gathered her into his arms.

Alexa caressed his thick, damp hair. "Jeremiah. J.J. I don't care who you are. Only that you belong to me now."

For a moment he remained silent, content to hold her and smell the musk of her body.

"Why didn't you tell me about your speech problem when we first met?" she asked.

For a moment he said nothing as he scraped his stubbled chin along her shoulder, the bristles abrading her flesh. It didn't hurt. She knew he felt an instinctive need to keep stamping his scent all over her.

"I'm an alpha," he finally said. "We're s-supposed to be perfect. Not damaged. Why I n-never could talk to w-women. Only men. Why I spoke in Spanish to you. Daniel and I used to be best buddies. I used to stammer when I was a child."

Alexa caressed his cheek. "You can speak in Spanish, if it makes it easier."

He shook his head. "Never again. F-from now on, it's only English around you. My f-father said I'd grow out of it. It was a sign that my wolf side was more dominant, but it made my life hell in school. D-daniel stuck up for me and then after school, he actually worked with me on my speech, teaching me to revert to Spanish to gain confidence. And then shortly after his 12th birthday, he changed. He started tormenting me. Salted my food, put hot sauce in my bed, teased me about being poor and my father not having money."

Her breath hitched. "Because Daniel had been possessed by the Changeling Gnome."

Staring at the sharp blue sky, he lowered his voice. "I suppose that is the real reason why I never told you the truth of who I was. I needed you to love me for who I really am, including my flaws. I'll never forget the hurt of Selena calling me a loser, but it's in the past now."

Alexa's heart turned over. She sat up and cupped his face in her hands. Such a strong, handsome face belonging to a male who had known such sorrow and rejection.

"You're no loser, J.J. Jeremiah. Juan. I can call you many names, but there's one I'm proudest of. *Mate*. And I love you. I can say it in Spanish, English, it doesn't matter, but you own my heart, forever."

He kissed her, his mouth warm and tender. Alexa knew as long as they were together, they would remain strong. Many obstacles awaited them, including raising Daniel, but together, they could face whatever came their way.

She had come to Jeremiah Jackson Taylor's bed a virgin hoping to win her freedom, and had become instead chained by her love for this male.

It was a prison Alexa never wanted to leave.

Ever.

BOOKS BY BONNIE VANAK

If you enjoyed this book, look for others in my Werewolves of Montana series.

Prequel: The Mating Heat

Book 1: The Mating Chase

Book 2: The Mating Hunt

Book 3: The Mating Seduction

Book 4: The Mating Rite

Book 4.5: The Mating Intent, Sienna's story

Book 5: The Mating Challenge, Aiden's story,
coming soon

Book 6: The Mating Season, Tristan's story,
coming soon

Book 7: The Mating Game, Gideo's story,
coming soon

Book 8: The Mating Ritual, Xavier's story,
release date TBA

BONNIE VANAK

Mating Minis set within the
Werewolves of Montana world

SEDUCTION

PASSION

OBSESSION

www.Bonnievanak.com

And be sure to check out OBSESSION, the next Mating Mini. Sexy Raphael finds the fiery redhead Jessica irresistible. But when he joins her on a search for her long-lost brother, Jessica doesn't realize Raphael has more than a happy family reunion in mind....

Turn the page for an excerpt from

OBSESSION

Werewolves of Montana series
Mating Mini #2

BONNIE VANAK

Coming January 2015

CHAPTER 1

New Mexico, seven years ago

Someone please get me the hell out of here. Please.

Raphael Amador gripped the iron bars of the cage until his knuckles fisted white. Sweat streamed down his temples, matting his long black hair and cutting rivulets through the dirt and caked blood on his naked body.

Four days, he silently chanted. Four more days in this hole and he'd be free.

Free? Hell, he'd be dead if he didn't find a way to escape.

For six days, they'd kept him in this cage in an abandoned animal testing facility. Scraps of moldy bread for food. A bucket in one corner to relieve himself and a fouled water dish in another. They wanted him drinking on his hands and knees, like a dog.

Raphael tried again to tug free the collar around his neck that prevented him from shifting in wolf. The leather and iron held fast. Infused with a strong warding, he could not break the restraint.

Imprisoned by one of his people and betrayed by his

196

own brother. He'd been a fool to trust Mary and her mate, Jules, when they begged for sanctuary in his pack two months ago.

He should have left them to rot by the roadside where he'd found them. But no, he had a soft spot for Lupines in trouble.

"Please, we need a safe haven. Please, my mate is sick and needs help," Mary had pleaded.

He didn't want to take them into his pack. Instinct warned they were not sincere. But his only brother, Angelo, insisted they were "good people."

And then one night as he'd slept, Angelo used the code only he and the pack beta possessed to unlock Raphael's house. Mary and Jules brought in their army of Others, killed Raphael's beta and several others before the reminder of his pack managed to escape.

In thanks for his assistance, Jules killed Angelo, too. His brother would never rule the pack as Jules had promised.

Raphael's chest tightened as he remembered the screams of the innocent mothers and young as they were slaughtered. He'd fought with all his might to get to his people, but the army of gnomes had proved too much. He'd promised to protect his pack from all harm, had vowed it as their alpha.

He'd failed.

Nothing would ever bring them back. *I'm sorry I wasn't there to keep you safe. I'm so sorry.*

Jules captured Raphael and left him alive for shits and giggles…as a reward for his followers. "If you can survive the cage for ten days, I'll set you free," Jules had told him.

I can do this. I can do this. Ride through the pain.

197

Pretend it doesn't exist. No emotions. Can't think of those I lost. Have to focus.

During the last session, he'd nearly passed out, but forced himself to stay conscious. If he fainted, he was dead.

Raphael didn't plan to die today, or tomorrow. *I can make it through.*

Four more days and he'd find a way to break free. Soon as Jules opened that cage door, he'd be on him, tearing him the fuck apart. He didn't need his wolf for the job. He'd gnaw through the SOB's throat with his teeth.

I am Lupine. I am strong.

The door to the shed opened. Raphael squeezed his eyes shut as the blinding New Mexican sunlight flooded the darkened room. He blinked hard, knowing he must not show weakness. He was alpha, strong and powerful.

A low, nasty giggle echoed through the shack. Raphael's eyesight adjusted and he swallowed rage at the sight of the Lupine standing before him. Jules's green gaze met his as the Lupine squatted down to Raphael's level. Dressed in pressed gray trousers and a black shirt, Jules looked like preppy Lupine out for a stroll, except for that flaming mop of red hair.

Few Lupines had hair that color.

Sunlight winked in the clear crystals studding the purple suede belt around Jules's lean waist. Raphael sensed the crystals fed the Lupine's extraordinary, dark magick. The stones glowed purple when Jules used his powers to hurt Raphael.

Jules McLean. He would never forget the face, nor the name.

I will have at you, you son of a bitch. I am patient. One day...

"And there is the almighty, powerful Raphael. Look at you, you helpless animal." Jules grinned as Raphael lunged at him, only to be yanked back by the length of chain attached to his collar.

"Join me in here and I'll show you how helpless I am."

Jules sat on the floor and dread curled down Raphael's spine. When Jules stayed for a conversation, he stayed to watch.

And laugh...

"I'd rather stay and watch you with my little ones. They're hungry this morning. Very hungry."

"Why are you doing this?" Raphael did not ask because he was curious. He did it, as he did every time his captor drew near, to examine his enemy for weakness.

"Because I can."

"But you need your army to back you. You're too puny to fight for yourself."

The suggestion hit home, for Jules's lips drew together. Sore spot. The male was only five foot six, compared to Raphael's six foot four.

"We'll see how weak and puny you'll be after my followers are finished with you."

Raphael searched Jules's face, saw the pinched look around his eyes. The male was tired. Drained. Perhaps controlling an army of gnomes taxed him more than he'd realized. A weakness...

He'd tested out the length of chain. All he needed was one shot at him.

"I survived. Doubt you would if they turned on you,

Jules. Jules. What kind of wuss name is Jules? Sounds like a girly girl name for a pussy-whipped Skin. 'Jules, don't play with those big boys, they might be too rough. You're too delicate for a Lupine, Jules.'"

Crimson flushed Jules's cheeks. His mouth turned down like a child denied a toy. *A little closer, just a little closer...*

Jules brought his face close. "You bastard. It's an honorable name, a name passed down by my father...I'll show you who's delicate."

He reached through the cage.

Gotcha!

Raphael sprang forward, seized Jules's hand and yanked hard. Jules banged his head against the iron bars, but then the crystals on his belt glowed purple.

Burning pain engulfed Raphael's fingers. He tried to hold onto Jules's hand, but the heat grew too intense. Cursing, Raphael drew back and Jules scuttled away, rubbing at his head.

"Just for that, you'll get an extra hour with the gnomes," he rasped.

His captor fished a remote out of his trouser pocket. "My gnomes are very hungry. And since you're a pureblood alpha, you heal quickly."

The iron door separating his cage from the one next door opened. Raphael tensed.

He did not speak, but reserved all his strength to fight them as the gnomes fell upon him, their pointed teeth clicking together like razored castanets.

He fought with all his strength and might. He grunted as one or two gained the advantage and tore at his back, the tastiest flesh, Jules had told him.

An hour later, he screamed.

**_Look for OBSESSION,
coming January 2015!_**

Stay updated with previews of more Werewolves of Montana books by visiting my website, www.Bonnievanak.com and signing up for my newsletter. Or visit my Facebook page at www.facebook.com/bonnievanakauthor.

ABOUT THE AUTHOR

Bonnie Vanak is the *New York Times* bestselling author of paranormal werewolf romances. A former newspaper reporter who became a writer for a major international charity, she travels to destitute countries to write about issues affecting the poor. Her books take readers from the mysterious, dark alleys of New Orleans to the sweeping plains of Montana. Visit her Web site at www.bonnievanak.com or email her at bonnievanak@aol.com.

Made in the USA
Coppell, TX
25 June 2020

29364259R00115